SHE'S
WITH
THE
BAND

GEORGIA CLARK

ALLEN&UNWIN

For Alecia, Danielle, Peter and Sarah

Allen & Unwin
83 Alexander St
Crows Nest NSW 2065
Australia
Phone: (61 2) 8425 0100
Fax: (61 2) 9906 2218
Email: info@allenandunwin.com
Web: www.allenandunwin.com

ISBN 978 1 74237 763 6

Design based on cover design by Tabitha King and Kirby Stalgis
Text design by Kirby Stalgis
Set in 12.5/16 pt Spectrum by Midland Typesetters, Australia
Printed in China at Everbest Printing Co.

10 9 8 7 6 5 4 3 2 1

1

Life never starts when you think it will. When I turned fifteen, I figured I'd be tossed the keys to the city, make out with a hottie, and have a modest parade thrown in my honour. But all that happened was that I got out of doing the washing up.

My dad's life didn't really start until about six years ago when he painted this huge, ridiculously ugly portrait of yours truly, won a big international art prize, stopped being Dad and started being 'world-renowned artist Sal Mannix', and suddenly became *the* person to say you met at parties.

The day we moved to Sydney was supposed to be the start of the new Mia Mannix – confident, charming, taller. But so far, it sucked.

Gaolbreak from my one-trick-pony town buried deep in the Snowy Mountains had finally begun pre-dawn. Clutching a thermos of hot tea, Dad and I drove silently up the main drag, cloaked in darkness – a movie set for the most boring film I'd *never* have to sit through again. Years of whingeing *will* pay off – don't let anyone tell you otherwise.

As the sun started to colour the landscape, anticipation clenched my belly like a slinky. Sin-city, here I come! There was only one thing missing: Cherry.

Fast-forward a few hours and the heat hit me like a prize-fighter when I scrambled out of the car at the truckstop Dad

1

had decided on for lunch. Soggy chips and a salad sandwich that'd had its glory days, a revival, published a tell-all auto-biography and *still* refused to die.

As I picked disinterestedly at it in our corner booth, I noticed Dad's lips were moving. Shrugging, I gestured to my headphones.

He leaned over and hit pause on my iPod. 'Perhaps we could have lunch without the racket, pet.'

'But this is my 'Lunch at a Truckstop' playlist. If I don't get through it now, it'll throw my whole afternoon schedule off.' I tossed him a sugar-sweet smile.

He eyed me, squeezing tomato sauce over his smelly sausage roll. 'Speaking of schedules . . .'

'Ooh, that's an exciting way to start a sentence . . .'

'I trust you're aware Silver Street High is going to be much more demanding than you're used to. You're won't have as much time for making playlists and reading *ENM*.'

I cocked an eyebrow at him. 'It's *NME*, Mr Dark Ages.'

He cleared his throat. 'How much did you get for Cherry?'

A pang hit me as I flashed on the ecstatic farm dude taking my baby from me. We'd been apart one week now, and it was hurting like a country and western megamix.

'Seven hundred and fifty dollars.'

He looked surprised. 'But it was second-hand.'

'She's a vintage Fender Stratocaster, Dad!' I exclaimed. 'That's a really good guitar!'

'Well, you'll need that money for art supplies, pet. They can really add up.' He took my hand. 'You won't regret this honey. I think you'll find the way art speaks to the soul a welcome change from all that yelling.'

My smile was paper-thin. 'Can't wait.'

It was late afternoon by the time we rolled into the driveway of our new postal: 15 Somerset Drive. An over-lipsticked real estate agent waved us in, gawking at me as I stumbled, stuffed with Snickers and legs aching, from the car.

'You must be Mia! I recognise you from your Dad's painting!'

She was one of those unflappable 'professional mum' types that advertisers use to sell chicken sauces and sunscreen. I'm vego, and burn faster than you can say 'melanoma'.

She flourished the house keys like a lucky door prize. 'Let me show you around!'

Ocean views a-go-go, and everything's made of grey glass and sparkling. Our pad was cookie-cutter new, empty (duh Mia) and soulless. Dad and I trailed the agent as she rabbited on about breezy, sun-drenched interiors and African quartzite floors.

'We are all so excited to welcome a great artist to the neighbourhood,' the agent enthused as we entered the stainless steel kitchen. The shiny surfaces reflected the three of us like funny mirrors at the circus. 'A real honour. It's strange though . . .' she paused to consider Dad with sharp thoughtfulness, 'you don't look famous, do you?'

I snorted laughter. Dad's a dead ringer for an unassuming high school cleaner. At his last exhibition opening, a mis-informed floor manager had him inspecting broken piping for ten minutes. My outburst was enough to make me the focus of her award-winning conversation skills.

'So, Mia. You must be so excited about starting at Silver Street tomorrow. Such a good school. Have you thought about what sort of extracurricular activities you'll be involved with?'

'Do you mean, like . . . homework?'

She laughed, exposing teeth the colour of liquid paper. 'I mean the Musical Society, Chess Club, Student Council, Social Committee . . .'

'Social Committee?' I shook my head, bewildered. 'I'm not joining a stupid Social Committee.'

Professional Mum stared at me with knives in her eyes, her voice dropping to a hoarse scary-serious whisper. 'The Social Committee is the backbone of the school. Without it, we'd have nothing.' She grabbed my shoulders, eyes boring into me freakily. '*Nothing!*'

The sound of a car approaching cut short the moment of total weirdness, catapulting Professional Mum back into character. 'That'll be the previous owners, the Ermans. Their daughter is a dance major at Silver Street! Come say hi!'

'Actually it's Cannon, not Erman. I'm not keeping my husband's name,' corrected the woman who shook Dad's hand. Make-up covered eyes with dark circles, and I recognised her from TV: a newsreader, I think. She looked me up and down carefully. I knew what she was thinking: *That girl from the painting is significantly uglier in real life.*

Everyone started signing official-looking forms as cicadas filled up the flat silence with their shrill salute to the oppressive heat. Sweat ran down my temples and I felt light-headed, sick. Social Committees? New friends? I had been so focussed on getting out of the Snowy that I hadn't really processed the fact that I was about to start at a strange school as a short, friendless nobody. The prospect felt like having to step onstage halfway through a musical you know nothing about and try to keep up.

I wanted to retreat to a bedroom I no longer had and mess round with a guitar I no longer owned. I wanted to be anywhere but here. And then, from the corner of my eye, movement. A flash of blonde hair followed by a pair of long legs emerging from the car's passenger side. The scratch of a match cued the poison smell of cig smoke.

While the rest of us had instinctively moved into the shade, the blonde slouched against the front of the house in the painfully blazing sun, letting it beat down, and burn — *bring it on*. Clad in a ripped denim mini and stained red heels, she kicked a stray stone. Mrs Cannon's dark circles had just gotten darker.

'If you want your allowance cut again this week, Lexie . . .' Mrs Cannon warned.

The girl sucked back insolently, and I realised I was staring. I looked quickly to the ocean — flat, distant, endless.

'This is Mia Mannix,' she continued, as if nothing was wrong. 'She'll be in your grade at school. Why don't you come say hello?' It was a request shot through with a plea.

Sighing slowly, the blonde click-clacked over, pushing sunglasses back to reveal messily mascaraed blue eyes flashing with a thousand secrets. I tried not to look scared. A smile flickered across lips smeared with blood-red gloss. When she spoke, her voice crunched sexy like the grey gravel underfoot.

'Just so you know — girl to girl — the black hole of sexual inexperience look isn't working for you.'

I blinked, confused.

Dad said, 'Oh.'

'Car. Now.' Mrs Cannon went red and fumbly. 'Mia, I'm so sorry, it's been a difficult move . . .'

Hasty awkward apologies continued as I shrugged off

5

Dad's attempt at a protective arm, my throat constricting. In the car the blonde sat low and stared straight ahead, arms crossed, the sunglasses mask revealing nothing. Well, at least I wasn't just Sal Mannix's daughter here. I was a black hole of sexual inexperience.

The great thing about being publicly humiliated is that people let you do whatever you like for the rest of the day, so I skulked downtown in search of a large, blunt weapon that'd fit in my school satchel. My list of things that Seemed Like A Good Idea At The Time (piercing my ears with a safety pin, practising making out with a pillow *without* locking my bedroom door et cetera) had a new top entry: moving to Sydney.

Catching a glimpse of myself in a shopfront window, I pulled a face at what made Lexie's lips curl. The girls here were tall, tan and stacked. I am short, slim and skim-milk pale: a vampire girl in Cons. Jet-black hair, which refuses to colour or curl, hanging in green eyes — not emerald, but not olive either. I always secretly fancied that Winona Ryder would play me in a movie, until my bratsville cousin told me it'd more likely be one of those hairless cats in a witch's wig. I told him he was adopted.

Rows of leafy outdoor cafes spilt over with botoxed ladies killing time before important fake-tan appointments. A lightly sweating couple in matching gym-wear jogged by, almost bowling me over without so much as a backward glance. A chihuahua gave me a death stare.

Maybe I really was made for tiny cold towns draped in fog and the smell of home-cooked food. Sydney was intense and intimidating, like a beauty queen on a bender.

I was just about to jump ship when I stumbled across a life raft: Shaky's.

Soundtrack: 'Seek Me', The Grates
Mood: Cautiously optimistic

'Band names these days are all about death and dying,' I'm saying, pacing the length of the poster-covered counter. 'The Kills, Death from Above 1979, The Fiery Furnaces . . .'

'The Killers, Death Cab for Cutie.' Mick, the wizened ex-rocker type who ran the place, poured me another black coffee.

'Die! Die! Die!' I grinned.

'Dead Disco, Dead Dead Girls . . .'

'You certainly seem to have all the answers, Mr Bond,' I drawled, tossing a stray stress ball in the air and catching it.

'I certainly do, Miss Moneypenny.' Upstairs an old phone started bleating. 'Watch the counter, kid. I gotta answer that'.

I tossed him the ball.

Record stores are to music junkies what all-you-can-eat buffets are to sumo wrestlers: a spiritual home. A hand-painted sign in dribbly red paint named this one Shaky's. And it was a good'un. Cardboard boxes of records rubbed shoulders with crates of CDs in the dingy clutter. On the shelves, Mick's favourite albums boasted lovingly written accolades slapped on their covers in a fine spidery print: *Delicate acoustic whimsy designed to break your heart in two and mend it by morning,* or *More dangerous than a hot-blooded cowboy finding his best friend's boxers under his tequila-soaked bed.*

Posters advertising upcoming gigs covered every bit of available wall space, while the front counter groaned under stacks of free street press and flyers.

7

In one corner, an open door revealed exciting things like mic stands and pools of cable: supplies for the rehearsal space upstairs.

Glancing at the rehearsal roster above the ancient cash register, I traced my finger down to the band in next: The Alaska Family. 'So, The Alaska Family, huh?' I called after Mick. 'Cute if slightly vacant 18-year-old trust-fund babies who mistook the invention of MySpace as an invitation to deliver their clichéd message of waa-waa teen angst?'

'You've heard of us.'

I spun around and gasped. Rock-and-roll perfection was right behind me. Everything about him — hair, clothes, body — was tousled, dark and loose. But it wasn't the guitar case and lead singer trappings that made hot hot heat rush up through my body. It was the gaze that met mine confidently — and didn't look away.

I stared back. Boys in the Snowy had buck teeth and farming aspirations. I had never seen someone so good-looking in real life. I half expected him to bust out a slogan for aftershave.

Instead, he smiled slowly, and reached out towards me. For a second I lost all logic and thought he was gonna pull me in for a pash . . . but instead his hand brushed the button badges on my dress that declared my devotion to The Shins and the Yeah Yeah Yeahs. I didn't know what to do, so I just raised my eyebrows.

'Nice badges. Haven't seen you in here before.'

'I just moved. Fifteen Somerset Drive.' Could he tell my knees were shaking?

'Lexie's old place? You're the artist's daughter?'

For once, the art freak-show thing didn't annoy me. Not when you can impress a crazily cute guy in under five minutes.

'I'm Mia.'

'Mia. Good to know there's fresh blood in town.' He shook my hand. His fingers were so warm and strong, I almost forgot to let go. 'I'm Justin. What school you at?'

'Silver Street High. Year Eleven.'

'I'm at Prince's College, Year Twelve, but my little sisters are in your year at Silver Street. Stacey and Sissy,' he grinned. 'They're officially pains in the ass as siblings, but they seem to party a lot.'

'Sure,' I said coolly, as if 'partying' was something I'd ordinarily be doing right now.

'Mr Jackson! Heads up.' Mick tossed a key over the counter.

'Thanks, Mick.' Justin winked at me and tapped his case. 'Someone told me it's, like, a long way to the top, so I'd better start climbing. See you round.'

'Sure,' I nodded, smiled, and then weirdly nodded again, watching Justin disappear up the stairs at the back of the shop. When I turned back to Mick he was looking at me with that painful 'knowing look' people use when they really don't know anything at all.

'Dad! *Dad!*'

His voice drifted up to my room, 'Downstairs, pet.' Then, as a wondered afterthought, 'We have a downstairs now . . .'

I leapt down the cream carpet stairs two at a time, bed-hair pulling off a just-electrocuted look nicely as I barrelled into the sun-drenched kitchen with the African quartzite floors.

'Where are my clothes?' Me, breathless.

'What, honey?' Him, clueless, elbow-deep in packing paper.

'Clothes, noun, plural: garments that cover the body.'

'Aren't they in your room in the box marked *clothes*?'

'That's winter stuff. Unless you want me to start at a new school this morning looking like I'm disguising a hideous skin disease . . . I need the box marked *Summer*.'

A connection sparked in Dad's eyes like a firework. 'Oh. Ooohh.' Then for good measure, 'Oh dear.'

'*Noooo*,' I breathed in an agonised whisper.

'Those boxes are still . . .'

'*Nooo* . . .'

'. . . in transit.' He waved a finger at me warningly. 'Now, don't overreact Mia.'

'Overreact?' I backed against the glass doors: a bunny in headlights. 'Overreact!'

'They'll be here tomorrow . . .'

'This is the worst possible thing that could happen to me!' My voice rose in sheer panic. 'What am I going to do?'

'Wear what you wore yesterday.'

I slumped down, head in hands. 'It's all in the wash.'

'You can wear my clothes.'

I looked up slowly and stared at him with dead eyes. 'Kill me now, Dad. Just kill me now.'

Soundtrack: 'It Ain't Funny How We Don't Talk Anymore', You Am I
Mood: Montage

In the brochures that arrived one foggy day last September (along with the acceptance letter Dad actually framed – gag), the school looked sunny, modern and full of an eclectic mix of dedicated over-achievers.

As I tried not to get in the way of boys on skateboards, and girls trying to catch the eyes of boys on skateboards, the school looked sunny, modern and full of an eclectic mix of dedicated over-achievers. I guess honesty is the best policy.

According to said brochures, Silver Street High was established to offer 'a university preparatory education to students planning for, or already pursuing, careers in performing arts or entertainment'. The 'already pursuing' part meant I recognised the girl whose locker was next to mine as Charlie Whitfield – a hot new actress who starred in a TV drama called *Cyber Rats*, where a motley crew of underground computer hackers fight evil in a dystopian cyberpunk future. Charlie's face pouted from the covers of countless chick magazines and I didn't even know which ones were cool.

As I struggled to make sense of my map, wacky boys with drumsticks loped past willowy girls stretching flawless figures poured into leotards. I was trying not to stare, but to act like the other kids did, 'This is my life, this is normal'.

Summoning every last ounce of courage, I gingerly tapped Charlie on the shoulder.

'Hey, um, I'm new and kinda lost. Can you show me where the . . .'

She whipped around, covering the phone with her hand. 'It's my manager,' she mouthed.

I scuttled away like a beetle in bad clothes.

'And then he was like, "Well, if you're not hanging with Richy, can I take you out for sangria?"'

'Like, what's sangria?'

'I think it's Mexican.'

'Um, excuse me?' I butted in. Two beautiful heads swished my way: a cherry redhead in a 'Bring The Noise' tight tee, and a Lucy Lui-esque girl in a cute plaid twin-set, who I recognised from some rather racy yoghurt ads.

'Um, can you tell me where the art rooms are? I'm new.' The girls let their eyes trail over me in disbelief as I attempted a look of nonchalant easy-breeze — *Yes, I am a teenage girl dressed like a 45-year-old man on welfare, but I don't have a problem with that*.

'What are you majoring in?' the red-head asked finally.

'Wait, let's guess,' interrupted Ms Yoplait. 'Hmmm . . . Too gawky for dance . . .'

'Too shy for acting,' continued Red, nodding. 'Music or Visual Arts. That outfit says Vis Arts.'

'Uh, yeah.' Perfect. I was officially a fashion disaster turned walking cliché.

'Wait a sec,' Red frowned in recognition. 'Are you Misha Mantle?'

'Mia Mannix.'

'That's what I meant.' She pointed a shiny pink nail at me. 'You're, like, the daughter of some super-famous painter. My brother told me about you!'

'Justin is such a hottie,' Yoplait drawled. 'Don't you guys end up making out when you're wasted?'

'Ewwww, Gillian!' shrieked Red, laughing. 'Don't listen to her, Mia, she's an idiot. My bro is so not cute, right?'

The guy would make Greek gods look plain. 'Um, I . . . don't know.'

'Articulate much?' smirked Yoplait, holding up some shiny strands of hair for inspection. 'I gotta ditch these split-ties before ID photos. Peace, you guys.' She sauntered off.

Red turned to me and smiled. 'I'm Stacey. C'mon. I'll show you where to go. Gillian's a dance major. She toured as an understudy with the Australian Dance Company last summer, and performed twice. That might sound like no big, but it totally is. Plus she's in a performance group I'm in – the Star Sisters. We're major.'

I nodded. 'Are you a dance student too?'

Stacey struck a pose. 'Acting, darling. I'm totally destined for silver screen success. Once I said, "Sure, that'd be great" on *Home and Away*. I was making this chick's boyfriend jealous.'

'That wouldn't be a stretch.'

She whirled around to face a buff, buzz-cut boy; basket-ball player's body covered by a *Save Water, Drink Beer* T-shirt.

'Can I help you, Carl?' Stacey's voice dripped scary sarcasm.

'C'mon Sissy, don't be ridiculous,' he smiled disarmingly. 'Meet me at the beach after school. The Milky Bars are on me.'

'Gee whiz, that'd be swell, but a) wrong twin, jerk, and b) sloppy seconds aren't *her* style.' Stacey glared poisonously at the dopey-looking Carl. 'Here're the art rooms, Mia. I'll see you later.'

In a haughty whirl of cherry red, she was gone.

'Okay, people! Listening caps on, motor mouths off! That means you Michael, Sarah!'

The teacher – a tall bespectacled British man in a coat and bow tie, glared in mock anger until the room settled. The large light-filled space resembled Dad's old studio: artworks-in-progress covered the walls, as did tins of paint oozing their insides and buckets of paintbrushes in varying states of decay. Books on technique and the 'way of the artist' were propped up against life-model mannequins and stacks of different sized canvases. Organised art chaos. Thankfully my weird old-man get-up didn't look completely fish-out-of-water compared to the experimental-art nerds filing in to find their seats.

'Right. For those new faces, I'm Mr Rochester – more commonly known as . . .' He waved for the class to answer.

'Rocho!' the class called, as if barracking at the footy.

'Right, very good,' continued Rocho, with a dry smile. 'And this year I'll be using the phrases: "I don't know art . . ."'

'. . . But I know what I pass,' the class chorused.

'And, "Rome wasn't built in a day . . ."'

'. . . But they didn't try hard enough.'

'Exactly. Now, that's a little about me, the rest I'm sure you can Google, like everyone else does.'

'When he was at art school he sold a painting of two dogs doing it,' whispered the girl next to me. 'We found it last year on eBay.'

Shocked, I choked on unplanned laughter.

'Excellent!' boomed Rocho. 'Our first new student has just volunteered to introduce herself.'

They say most people fear public speaking more than death. I fear public speaking more than waking up during open-heart surgery, finding out your boyfriend is really your brother AND accidentally vomiting on someone important, combined. Twenty sets of eyeballs watched me shuffle past to stand up the front.

'Hi, um, I'm Mia. Mia Mannix. I moved here yesterday with my dad . . .' A few kids nudged each other. 'And, um, it's really . . . hot here.'

'Duh,' someone muttered, and the class snickered.

Embarrassment burnt through me like bushfire, and I glanced at Rocho in a panic. He nodded for me to continue. I took a deep breath, desperate not to fail whatever personality test this was supposed to be.

'Look, you wanna ask about my dad, right? I don't really like talking about him 'cause it's weird, but if I were you and you were me, I guess I'd be curious. So, um, you guys can ask me anything you like now, but that's it for the rest of the year. Deal?'

The class looked at each other in confusion.

'Seriously.' Please let this pay off. 'Fire away.'

Nothing. Eyes darted sideways, trying to suss which way to play this. Still nothing . . . My forehead prickled with stress-sweat. C'mon . . . Then, finally, a long-haired boy up the back raised his hand.

'Where does he paint?'

'At our old place he made a big cattle shed into a studio, but here he's going to convert the guest wing of the house.'

Another hand. 'Does he paint all the time?'

'If he's working on something new or has a deadline for

something, he'll work all day and all night — and only sleep three or four hours. But sometimes he'll just spend the day reading and watching TV.'

'What does he watch?'

'The news, stuff on SBS,' I frowned. 'Oh, he loves those *Chaser* guys. He actually uses the word "scallywags" to describe them.'

The class laughed. Hands waved in the air as questions started flying from every corner.

'Is it true he's dating that actress, Radha Mitchell?'

I laughed. 'No, they were just photographed together at an opening.'

'So he's single?'

'Sarah!' Rocho quickly reprimanded the cheeky strawberry-blonde.

'No, it's cool,' I countered. 'Yeah, he is. I think he dug the real estate agent who sold us our house though. He said she was "very nice and welcoming", which I reckon is Dad-speak for "a total babe".'

'All right, go Sal!' yelled Sarah, and everyone laughed.

'Settle down, monkeys.' Rochester hopped off his desk. 'Mia's been very accommodating in entertaining your tiny, curious minds, but we stand at the brink of a new school year . . .'

'Just one more question, Rocho,' everyone called out. 'C'mon!'

'All right, all right. Miss Mia — last question please.'

I locked eyes with a lanky boy in black-rimmed glasses. 'Yeah?'

He cleared his throat. 'So, if you have kids, are you gonna paint their portraits or just stick to photographs like the rest of the world?'

I blushed and stared down at my sneakers. 'Um . . .'

He laughed nervously. 'Hey, I was kidding . . .'

'I didn't ask to have my portrait painted,' I found myself snapping. 'My dad's an artist, it's what they do.'

'Seriously, it was a joke . . .'

'Right, thank you, Mia,' Rochester threw the boy a bemused look. 'On that note, the school year begins . . .'

As I slid back into my seat, I snuck another look at the glasses boy. He could tell I was watching him, but he didn't look back. Weirdo, I decided. Mean, freaky weirdo.

Students swarmed like honeybees in designer threads to find a spot in the shade for our very first lunch. Don't let me sit on my own, I pleaded silently. Surely someone would wave me over, take pity on the new girl in the funny clothes.

Someone? Anyone . . . ?

Cursing my cowardly nature, I was just about to duck into the loos to hang with my friend Suds the Soap Dispenser, when I spotted a flash of red. Stacey! I fought the urge to scream her name with relief, and instead plonked down next to her and dug an apple out of my bag.

'How was your first class?' I spoke through a mouthful of juicy Granny Smith. 'Vis Arts wasn't bad. This semester is all "traditional skills and disciplines". Easy. Kinda boring though. I had to do Vis Arts to get Dad to agree to move to Sydney, but exactly how life-changing is still life, y'know?'

Stacey peered suspiciously over her sunglasses at me.

'What?' I asked. 'Do I have paint on my face?'

'Are you high?'

'Huh?'

'Are. You. High.'

17

'Oh, um, no thanks. I don't really do drugs. I mean, it's fine if you want to but . . .'

'Why are you talking to me?'

I choked on apple. 'What?'

'You're disconcerting.' She frowned delicately. 'You can leave now.'

'Okay,' I whispered. 'I'm sorry. I thought . . .'

'Don't think.' A smile as frosty as a strawberry slushie. 'Just leave.'

Hands shaking, I scooped up my satchel, ready to bail. But straightening up, I saw: 'Stacey?' Reality dawned.

'Hey, chick.' She blew me a kiss. 'I see you've met the less attractive Jackson. Yo, Sissy, you'll never guess who wants to hang out with *you* . . .'

Over sushi and sparkling mineral water, the Carl situation took front and centre. The facts as they stand: 1) Sissy and Carl used to have a thing. 2) While Sissy was away on a 'totally random' modelling shoot, Carl had a thing with someone else. 3) Sissy and Carl no longer have a thing.

Stacey spent approximately thirty-five minutes denouncing Carl as everything from 'an airhead with no licence' to 'a double-timing low-life who has more in common with a compost heap than the human race'.

Sissy responded to this by sighing and muttering 'chill out' and 'he just wants to *hang*' as Stacey started listing all the novelty T-shirts she'd seen him in that 'both sucked AND blew'. Sissy sat practically immobile, an ice statue in shades, moving only to shoot me steely glances, which said 'Who are you?' and 'Why are you here?' and 'Is that outfit ironic or just plain stupid?'.

Just as Stacey remembered a T-shirt which read *FBI: Female Body Inspector*, the hacky sack a group of kids had been kicking around arched high over their heads, coming to land neatly in Sissy's Caesar salad.

'Keep an eye on your balls, kid,' she snarled to the skittish skinny boy who came to collect it. 'You'll lose them'.

'Sorry.' He backed away sheepishly.

'You should be,' she muttered. 'I can't eat this now.'

'Get something tasty from the cafeteria,' Stacey offered, sucking red-rope liquorice provocatively.

'These damn heels give me blisters.' Sissy slipped them off, wincing. 'Can you go for me?'

'Oh, it'd be an honour, Your Majesty.' She bowed, smirking (a family trait).

'Mia,' the ice statue fixed her gaze on me, 'would you mind?'

Something passed between the twins.

'Um, okay.'

'Oh, isn't she a sweetheart?' Sissy cooed. 'Garden Salad – nix the dressing. Pay you back *mañana*.'

GARDEN SALAD NOT AVAILABLE.

Alarm bells stared to ring – literally, from a car outside – and then stopped.

But the offending sign still stared me in the face. Tuna and Greek Salads were nestled happily in their see-through plastic beds, stacked high next to Garden Salad's empty row. I rubbed my forehead, feeling a lettuce-related headache seep through the back of my skull.

'Tough call, huh? Tuna or Greek.' The glasses-wearing art-class boy had appeared at my elbow. 'Need a hand deciding?'

'What, should I paint their pictures?' My words were tart. 'Thanks, I can handle this.'

He flicked me an amused smile and began commentating into an imaginary microphone. 'Folks, tonight's match is proving to be a doozy. In the red corner we have Greek Salad: the sharp salty goodness of olive and feta cheese calmed by robust sweet tomato. And in the blue corner, Tuna Salad: chunks of flavoursome sea life, enveloped in naughty-but-nice mayonnaise. The gloves are off in the battle of healthy lunch options at Silver Street High.'

'I said I didn't need your help,' I said sharply, refusing to be amused.

Unperturbed, he shoved the microphone in my face. 'Mia Mannix, from your position ringside tell the folks at home who you think will take the crown.'

'I . . . I don't know.' I imagined Sissy's cold disapproval of either choice, eyes flashing like a pirate's cutlass catching the moonlight before claiming a life. 'I need a Garden one!'

'Mia, the words "it's only salad" are flashing above you in large neon letters.'

'You don't understand!' I wailed. 'If I buy the wrong one . . .'

'Okay, okay!' Hands waved to quell my outburst. 'Look, I bought a Garden Salad yesterday and only had a few bites 'cause it lacked charisma and charm. Let's buy a Greek Salad, fill out my Garden Salad, and ta-da! One Super Salad Solution.'

I couldn't help but crack a smile. Boy Wonder dipped his head in the direction of some stairs. I found myself falling in step beside him.

He walked with the deliberate quickness of a cat on a kill. Sneaking a glance at his face, I got the distinct impression of self-assured intelligence, a million thoughts jostling under the surface. His eyes darted to take in the content of every poster pinned to the noticeboards and the details of every person we passed. It felt as if we were on a spy mission.

'Here we are.' He stopped, stuck a key in a door covered with faded stickers, and peered at me through narrowed eyes. 'Can you keep a secret?'

'No complaints so far.' Okay, so I'd never had anyone to keep secrets for, but that sounded cooler.

'Excellent.'

The door swung open to reveal a windowless room crammed with junk of all shapes and sizes: mad scientist's lab meets burgled op-shop. Stuffed red parakeets regarded me from a swinging wooden cage, while a mound of expressionless mannequins lay disinterestedly in a heap. Stacks of ancient magazines were piled haphazardly on top of the computers in the corner, threatening to topple with the faintest breeze. Old movie posters were Blu-tacked clumsily to the wall – swooning French lovers frozen in infatuation and impassioned martial-arts men sworn to bloody revenge.

A whiteboard with dates and deadlines scribbled on it seemed to be the only thing representing any kind of order.

'Welcome to my office.' The boy hastily swiped some empty takeaway containers into an overflowing bin. 'Actually, it's the school newspaper's office but given it's a one-man-show, I claim it as my own. Emil Allen, editor extraordinaire.'

I gestured to the picture that hung above his desk: a large, black-and-white photograph of two naked women, both covered in paint, one dragging the other across a big canvas in front of an audience of well-dressed onlookers. 'Jugs out for art. Is this the secret that gets you through the day?'

He glanced at the picture, unsure if I was impressed or offended.

'That's Yves Klein. French guy. Used to make artworks by using, ah, human paintbrushes.' He shot me a furrowed-brow look. 'I thought you'd be into artists like him. I mean, your dad . . .'

'. . . Uses stock-standard, totally inanimate paintbrushes,' I quipped. 'So where's this secret?'

He whistled. 'Libby! We have company.'

A tiny brown puppy emerged from a pile of cushions, yawning.

'Omigod, a puppy!' I squealed. She tumbled over to Emil, yapping until he scooped her up. 'Shhh,' he repri-manded her gently. 'Stealth-like, remember? We're in enemy territory.' She sneezed and looked up at Emil in surprise. 'I found her a few days ago in a cardboard box. I think someone was trying to get rid of her.'

'Wow, that's a real lose-faith-in-humanity moment.' Warm little licks covered my hand. 'She's so cute.'

'Hold her. I'll fix you that salad.'

She settled into my arms, pillow-soft and puppy-fat.

'So, who ya buying lunch for?' he asked. 'Hot date?'

'Sissy Jackson.' Whose brother is the hottest date in the world, I added silently.

'Really?' He glanced over at me in surprise.

'What?'

'Nothing . . .'

'C'mon, what?'

'Nothing!'

'Don't make me hurt zee puppy,' I busted out my best Russian bad guy accent.

'It's just . . . those girls have more agendas than the UN.' He sealed the made-over salad and slid it into a paper bag.

I rolled my eyes. 'Lemme guess – the popular girls are the bitchiest? I've seen that movie. But they're the only people who've actually talked to me.'

He raised his eyebrows at me. His eyes were the same colour as mine – green. Not emerald, but not olive either.

'Okay, okay,' I conceded. '*You're* talking to me too.'

'Plus, their "band" sucks in a mind-blowingly awful way. When I think about their last few shows . . .' he shuddered. 'Let's just say my therapist thinks I still have a long way to go. Anyway, you'd better get going.'

He grinned as he pulled open the heavy door for me. 'If Sissy gets upset, she sheds her human skin and starts eating babies.'

The end-of-lunch, beginning-of-assembly bell was ringing as I raced back to double trouble.

'Sorry, I got talking to Emil someone-or-other,' I apologised, offering Sissy the salad. 'You guys know him?'

'No,' Sissy muttered, opening the bag sceptically.

'Yes, we do,' exclaimed Stacey. 'He interviewed us last year for the school paper – that story about twins having ESP.'

'Oh yeah.' Sissy addressed with me with authority. 'He tested us and it turns out we have it. ESP. Extra Special Privilege. I guess it just goes with being a twin,' she shrugged, sniffing. 'Mia, you smell weird. Like a dog.'

The girls dissolved into giggles as we were instructed to make our way to the quadrangle for assembly.

As the headmistress, Mrs Kapranos, an elegant if intimidating woman in her fifties, rambled on about welcoming us all to another exciting school year, Yoplait (Gillian) squeezed down next to us, receiving a disapproving glare from Mr Rochester. Her apologetic smile morphed into a snarl as soon as he turned his back.

'I heard they asked Nicole Moretti to be Head Girl for our year,' Gillian murmured to Stacey. 'After You Know Who got busted.'

Stacey nodded, glancing nervously at her twin, who was absorbed in writing a text.

'They kicked, ah, You Know Who off Social Committee too,' Stacey whispered back. 'I haven't seen her all day . . .'

'It's cool, guys.' Sissy snapped her phone shut, her voice bright and hard. 'You can say her name in front of me.' She raised her voice defiantly. 'Lexie: the cow who screwed my boyfriend!'

'That is *enough*.' Rocho glared fiercely at us. 'Another word and you can continue this conversation in detention.'

Apologies were mumbled with faux-humility as we turned our attention to the front.

'A reminder: your Battle of the Band entries are due tomorrow. Quiet, please.' Mrs Kapranos waved down the whistles and yelps. 'The music staff will choose four bands from the entries submitted. Those four bands will then play in Silver Street High's official heat. The winner of the heat will play in the state final. Direct any questions to the coordinator, Mrs Prisk, after assembly'. A severe-looking woman with a cat's bum mouth nodded at us primly.

'Star Sisters are gonna *clean up*,' Stacey grinned at the others, and the three slapped hands.

'The Year 11 Head Girl has had to step down for personal reasons,' Mrs Kapranos continued. 'Therefore we've asked Nicole Moretti to take up the position. Nicole?'

Bodies rustled as necks craned.

'Nicole?' Mrs Kapranos asked into the microphone. 'I spoke to her this morning . . .'

'I'm here.'

Eyes turned to the back of the assembly to follow the assertive voice.

'No. Freakin'. Way.' said the twins in unison.

Strutting down the centre of the assembly like it was a Milan catwalk, was sex itself. Glossy chestnut-brown hair slipped and slid off tan shoulders, tickling a plunging neckline. Boobs jiggled. Hips wiggled. Boys whistled and the twins' jaws hit the floor.

The girl took her place at the microphone, letting a slow smile grow as she scanned the waiting assembly.

'What happened to netball skirts and greasy hair?' exclaimed Stacey.

'*Damn*, she got some wicked style.' Sissy turned to Gillian and gave her a once-over. 'Sorry, babe. Star Sister's line-up just changed.'

'What?' Gillian gawked. 'Are you for real!? I spent all summer learning those routines! Stace?'

Stacey studied her manicure intently, as Gillian's eyes burnt with girl fury.

'Hate the game, not the player,' Sissy purred.

Gillian grabbed her clutch and stormed off. Sissy sighed delicately. 'Survival of the fittest, Mia. Live and learn.'

If a warlock cast a spell on a wayward magpie, ordering it to instruct children on the ways of the written word, that'd be our English teacher, Mrs Metcalf. She was small and shrunken, her black hair pulled into a tight bun. Older than your mum, younger than your gran, she hopped about the classroom excitedly.

'This is such a waste of time,' Sissy moaned. 'Seriously,

how is learning about some dead guy's plays gonna help me score a role opposite Channing Tatum?'

'Who's Channing Tatum?' I asked.

Sissy looked at me as though I'd just offered to amuse her by eating my own head.

'*Hamlet!*' Mrs Metcalf warbled. 'Shakespeare's most famous play. A tale of bloody revenge, terrible tragedy, supernatural intervention and . . .'

The classroom door swung open, and there, with the sun streaming in behind her, stood Lexie. She was dressed in the same clothes she'd worn yesterday, but now they were crumpled, like she'd slept in them.

Nudges and glances swept through the room. Sissy stiffened.

Mrs Metcalf addressed the latecomer dryly, 'Lexie. So glad you could join us.'

Lexie slid into the last seat, a few rows over from us.

'Right,' Metcalf continued. 'I trust you've all read the play over summer.'

'*Tramp,*' Sissy coughed deftly into her hand, causing a stronger ripple to run through the class.

Lexie stared ahead, seemingly impervious as Mrs Metcalf twittered on, 'Tell me about it. Hands in the air, please.'

We shifted in our seats: inmates unwilling to squeal.

Michael from art class raised his hand. 'I subscribe to the Homer Simpson theory. That *Hamlet* was made into *Ghostbusters*. That's right, isn't it?'

We sniggered, and Metcalf frowned. 'Anyone else?' Yes, Lexie?'

The girl in question stuck her chin out. 'I feel sorry for Ophelia. She's into Hamlet but he's *so* not into her.' She looked directly at Sissy, her voice soaked in scorn. 'It's like her only worth or purpose is defined by guys. And then she drowns herself. That's so sad.'

Metcalf nodded enthusiastically, unaware of Sissy's seething. 'Very interesting observation, Lexie. Ophelia is torn between the demands of her father and the demands of Hamlet. You could say she sees her value determined by their approval. Yes, Sissy?'

'Mrs Metcalf, is it true Ophelia and Hamlet were lovers?'

'It's hinted at,' Metcalf chose her words carefully, 'but the nature of their relationship is never made clear. It's up to your interpretation.'

'Really?' replied Sissy innocently. 'I thought everyone knew she was sleeping around.'

Someone up the back laughed, quickly turning it into a cough. Sissy caught Lexie's eye. Smiling prettily, she slid her middle finger delicately across her throat and held it up in Lexie's direction. Lexie snarled back, ready for a fight.

Something was *definitely* rotten at Silver Street High . . .

I lay on my bed, amidst half-built bookshelves and packing boxes spewing dog-eared music magazines, and reread the invitation for the thousandth time.

Rule the School Pool Party. Tonite, 6 p.m. till late. BYO. <u>*Invite only*</u>*!!*

And then the bit that made me feel like throwing up and climbing every mountain, both at once:

Luv Sissy, Stacey + Justin.

The afternoon sun beat down in stubborn opposition to the black cloud that'd settled in my room. I had outfit issues. My attempt at making men's shirts and grandpa hats hip may have flown in art class, but there was no way that'd pass at a party that promised to be overflowing with cold booze and hot guys. Clothes maketh the teen and, like Mother Hubbard, my cupboard was bare.

Defeated, the invite sailed towards the bin as I reached for Cherry – in times of need we made a good team. And then it hit me: Oh yeah. No Cherry. I wasn't allowed to play guitar anymore. I'd swapped passion for a postcode, but I was beginning to think I'd done a deal with the devil disguised as my dad.

I flopped back on my bed in sheer frustration – but as I did, a solution suddenly and clearly presented itself. Of course!

Party round the back y'all!

The handwritten sign led me round the side of a large

blonde-brick house, in the direction of sexy-as electro beats — the soundtrack to so many imaginary parties I'd never been invited to. Catching a glimpse of myself in a side window, I ripped off a stray price tag and couldn't help but grin, lips sticky with Very Berry Jelly Gloss. *I made it. I was here.*

I'd never worn heels before, making the wobble factor medium to high, but I figured I could fake a strut. I had exactly five hours before Dad said he'd be back from his meeting with some art gallery curator — plenty of time to begin my new life.

Breathing deeply, I repeated the magazine mantra: confidence, confidence, confidence. I am Mia Mannix, teen goddess.

Soundtrack: 'Saturdays', Cut Copy
Mood: Intimidated

If this party was a sexual preference, it'd be SWINGER.

Girls in teeny-weeny polka-dot bikinis let their hips scoot and sway, sneaky smiles playing on their lips. Two boys with tattoos snaking up their backs arm-wrestled, as someone bombed into the pool to a chorus of squeals from the brown surfer chicks lounging in caps and cut-off cargos. A mound of seafood salad had been attacked, prawns hanging helpless in the late afternoon sun, while sausages sizzled on a barbeque, filling the warm air with their rich salty smell. It was right in front of me but it felt untouchable.

The double glass doors led to an open-plan kitchen, and lounge room full of stoner boys smoking potent bubbling bongs and lolling about watching skate videos.

'Mia!' A sailor-capped Stacey smooched my cheek, all vodka and lipstick, looking me over in surprised approval. 'Cute outfit.'

29

'Fashion is a form of ugliness so intolerable, we have to alter it every six months,' I offered airily. She stared at me as if I'd just slapped her in the face.

'Oscar Wilde,' I added quickly. 'Famous . . . gay guy.'

'Oh. Right.' She smiled non-comprehendingly, sloshing pink liquid into a glass. 'Cosmo?'

Hesitation. Dad let me have a glass of champagne at his exhibition openings, but I rarely did – drunk daughter of the painter is not a good look.

'Cosmo.' The question became a statement of instruction, and as if on autopilot, I complied.

'Thank you.' Mmm . . . yum. Turns out, pink is a pretty nice flavour.

'Gonna take a dip?'

'I, uh, forgot my swimmers,' I lied. I'd be mistaken for Casper the Friendly Ghost next to the babes on patrol outside.

Stacey nodded conspiratorially, fluffing her sleek crimson waves. 'Check. Me and Sissy just maxed out our Visas at Toni & Guy, so it's no water sports for us either.'

'Oh, yeah, your hair looks really great.' It looked exactly the same as it did at school. Stacey smiled brightly as a curly-haired boy grabbed her bum, grunting like a Neanderthal. She shrieked, he chased her outside, and I wondered how far evolution had really gotten us.

A polite smile plastered my mouth. I sipped and swilled, trying to look cool and casual, and not (as instructed by the magazine mantra) desperate or needy, which was exactly how I felt. Ten minutes crawled by. After reapplying fresh Very Berry Jelly Gloss and pretending to receive and send several hilarious text messages to absent friends, I was running out of defence mechanisms. It was time to bite the bullet and talk to someone.

'Hey, um, hi.' I smiled hopefully at a slouchy-cool girl wearing Mickey Mouse ears.

'Playing the field is so disgusting. Think about what a field is: it's an overgrown cesspool of dirt, dog poo and the excesses of a depraved drug-and-junk-food-driven society. How is the field a good place to be?' She took a long swallow of a beer, and looked at me.

I cleared my throat. 'Do you know where the bathroom is?'

'Babe, you're know you're the only one for me.' Carl's eyes grazed Sissy's rack with the subtlety of a marching band.

'What evs,' sighed Sissy, feigning boredom but making no move to leave.

'C'mon Sis . . . It's been *ages* . . .'

Ducking past the overtures of re-ignited passion, I made my way upstairs. Each door on the second floor looked exactly the same. I opened one at random: lemon-fresh linen closet. I gently opened another. The afternoon light barely penetrated the darkened room. Clothes littered the floor, a guitar case lay open on an unmade bed. It smelt vaguely like aftershave and shoes: a boy smell. I started to close the door and move on, but sometimes self-control just packs up and says adios.

Tacked to a corkboard were a few happy-snap photos: one of which I assumed was the band, sleepy hotties sprawled at an airport. A few geeky ones of the twins as unself-conscious kids, squealy-happy and playing in mud – undoubtedly pictures they now hated. And finally one of Justin, in a tux, glancing at the camera in annoyance. The photo was ripped down the middle – the other half missing. I traced my finger down the rip, wondering what story it told. Muffled footsteps outside the door cut short my ponderings. I spun around, trapped. The door opened slowly, as part of a conversation spilled into the room.

'Dude, chill, I'm not saying it's not a good song. It's just . . . not a good song.'

Keys and smokes crashed onto a shelf.

'I dunno. Get high. Get laid.'

Heart pounding, I shrank back into the corner of the room and ducked behind a clothes rack. An old leather jacket brushed against my cheek and I inhaled its rich, dark smell giddily.

'Yeah, cool. *Mañana.*'

Phone shoved in back pocket, Justin flopped onto his bed, stretching and groaning, biceps bulging *just enough* at the sleeves. A tattoo of music notes encircled one arm. He unbuttoned his jeans. *He unbuttoned his jeans.* No. Oh no. One hand started to slide down his chest and he exhaled noisily. He reached into his pants and groaned. I felt hot and faint, prickly, rooted to the spot, unable to move, flushed red.

Then he looked directly at me.

'First five minutes free. After that you gotta flash some cash.' And he was up, striding towards me, parting the clothes on the rack. 'Mia Mannix. We meet again.'

Soundtrack: Red Riders, 'Slide In Next To Me'
Mood: Feeling it

Sexy basslines were kicking in, and he couldn't believe I hadn't smoked pot before.

'What did you do for kicks in — wait, where'd you ship in from?'

I perched awkwardly on the corner of his bed.

'The Snowy Mountains. It's a watching-paint-dry kinda place. Literally.' *Wait, was that too my-dad's-a-famous-artist? He probably thinks I'm totally lame. And desperate. And . . .*

'So, the move to Silver Street: spread your wings, meet new friends, let them corrupt you?'

'Something like that.' My heart was hammering so hard we should've been wearing construction hats and ear plugs.

He lit up, fire illuminating his face briefly with a devilish glow. 'I like it.' He passed me the joint.

'Oh, actually, no thanks.' I felt wobbly enough from the Cosmos I'd been sucking back. Even the pungent smell of the smoke made me feel less than super.

'Are you sure?' He leaned towards me, heavy-lidded eyes locked intensely to mine, full of promise and adventure. I froze, staring back. Was I supposed to . . . Was this going to be . . . Suddenly the door burst open — needle jerking off a record. A leopard-print bikini bod dripped wet on his carpet.

'Smells like teen spirit.' Hands twitched on hips.

Justin's eyes widened. '*Nicole*?'

'Bingo bango, Jackson.' She flopped onto the bed between us, water beads glistening on a too-flat stomach. 'But it's Nikki now. Is the next toke taken or what?'

'All yours, babe.' He put the joint between her lips, gazing at her in fascination as she inhaled deeply, cat-eyes closed. The scene had become a dictionary definition of 'third wheel' and a wave of paranoia started to rise up from my feet. I felt like a $2 shop ornament: ugly, cheap, out-of-place.

'Mia, right?' Nikki turned to me. 'How do you know Justin?' Her tone was friendly but her eyes were hard.

'We, um . . . met in a record store.' Words were dumb and stiff in my mouth as Nikki's amused face blurred in front of me.

'*Fascinating.*'

Justin pushed his hair out of his eyes, as they broke speed limits racing over wet curves. 'So, Nikki, did you, um, go away over summer or . . .'

Her laugh tinkled easily. 'Italy. My aunt's a fashion designer over there – she spoilt me rotten. Whole new wardrobe – blah, blah, blah.'

My aunt lives in Dubbo and teaches kindergarten kids. If I'm good, she buys me toffee apples.

Miss Italian Makeover went to pass me the joint. Justin stopped her. 'Mia doesn't smoke.'

'Actually, why not,' I interrupted. Two could play at this game. I leant over Nikki, towards Justin. 'Hook me up.'

Hot harsh smoke hit the back of my throat as I sucked back, hard. My eyes stung with tears and I struggled not to cough – no such luck.

Nikki giggled as my spluttery heaves finally subsided. She sat up to face Justin, giving me a great view of her smooth, evenly tanned back. 'I know it's *tres* juvenile, but the kids have started Spin the Bottle. Are you game or lame?'

Does a starving man want a sandwich?

Soundtrack: 'Robocat', teenagersintokyo
Mood: Things are blurry

A mix of smells hit me as we trooped down to the ground floor: burnt barbeque, cig smoke, spew. Flesh bumped and spilled everywhere, and the noisy, packed lounge room was moving, unstable. Music shrieked from a stereo and everyone's faces were twisting, turning demented, animalistic and weird. My forehead prickled hotly as I leant against a doorway, trying hard to get a grip. Carl and Sissy come into focus, feverishly devouring each other in the kitchen, mouths a mash of twisting tongue.

Sissy clocked my glazed stare. 'What do you want, a threesome?'

Carl whipped round. 'For real? Killer!'

'Hey!' She swatted him sharply. 'I wasn't serious!'

'How am I supposed to know you're joking . . .'

'We're back together five minutes and you wanna be with someone else, how unpredictable . . .'

'Sissy, come back – *Sissy!*'

'C'mon guys, it's started.' Nikki pulled me and Justin into a circle of unfamiliar, pulsating faces as an empty vodka bottle spun to Stacey. The kids hooted and she leant over to suck face with an eager, thick-lipped boy.

The room tipped, and I closed my eyes to stop it.

'Mia!' Stacey and Nikki screeched in unison, laughing hysterically. Why was the bottle now facing me? Confused, I glanced instinctively to Justin, who was looking at someone hovering over me. A sweaty, red-faced boy leered at me, ripe breath stinking of pork sausages. Without thinking, I scooted back on my hands, knocking over a mug of dark red goon, which landed half on me, half on the carpet. Over a string of expletives from the twins, I pushed my way out of the circle, out of the lounge room, out, out, away.

I stumbled out beside the pool and sank into a shadowed corner. The line from a bad review of one of Dad's art shows echoed endlessly in my poisoned brain: *The trouble with testing limits is sometimes you find them.*

Taking deep breaths, I rubbed my leaky eyes as the stars dipped and raced above me. I wanted my dad. I wanted to be back in our old cosy cottage overlooking the foggy valley, sitting cross-legged on the woolly rug in front of the fire, letting my fingers find chords and riffs with Cherry. Jazz records spinning scratchily, crossword puzzles half-done on our big oak table, Dad absentmindedly chopping carrots . . .

Double trouble jolted me back to Planet Twin.

'. . . her problem? Weird much?'

'She's totally frigid. I bet she hails from Virginia.'

'Deffo. She gives off so many never-been-laid vibes I feel like *I'm* a virgin.'

'What's the deal, ladies?' asked Nikki, inspecting her reflection in the glass doors. 'I didn't get the BYO loser memo.'

Someone snorted. 'It's her dad. He's like . . .'

'Totally famous. It's called networking, duh!'

Nikki sniffed, 'You'd have to be on ice if you think that sad little nobody could ever give anyone a leg up. She's too busy trying to get a leg over my next boyfriend. Now, if *I* was a TDF rock star, who would I go for: nervy nerdling or Sassy Star Sister . . .'

The twins joined in: 'Ugly duckling or the swan?'

'Mousy Mia or—'

'Okay, enough!' I yelled. The three jumped, as I stumbled towards them. 'What about Stuck-Up Nikki? Staggeringly Superficial Nikki? Oh, my bad,' I sighed. 'I probably should be using words with fewer syllables, shouldn't I?'

'Who the hell do you think you are,' Nikki snarled.

'Who the hell do you think *you* are?' I exclaimed, words spitting easily from lucid lips. 'What, you go through a holiday makeover to become the school's biggest bimbo? And you two,' I shook my head in disbelief, 'you make friends

36

with me because you think my dad can get you a "foot in the door"? Hate to bust your bubble, but my dad's actually talented. He didn't get where he is today by being a big flirt in a short skirt.'

'What would you know about talent or flirting?' sneered Sissy. 'You can't even handle a party pash. I bet no one's been wasted enough to kiss you.'

Tongue-tied, I rolled my eyes.

'Omigod, it's true,' Sissy gasped. 'You're a pash-virgin.'

Nikki stepped forward. 'You are the most pathetic person I've ever met.'

A wave of rage swept over me, and I started running — not away, but at them. I shoved Nikki hard and she tottered backwards, clutching at Stacey who grabbed at Sissy. A squealing mess and *splash*! The Star Sisters crashed backwards into the pool!

'You cow!' they screamed, flailing helplessly. 'You're *dead*!'

Eyes and mouth open wide I backed away, a laugh fighting its way up my throat. I spun around to see the entire party staring at me, their faces a mixture of shock, disgust and glee. So I did what any strong, proud girl would do at that moment: I piss-bolted.

It wasn't the snickering and sideways glances that started as soon as I stepped through the school gates that broke me. It wasn't discovering a selection of words that definitely *weren't* G-rated scrawled across my locker. I even kept my cool when everyone blanked me at recess, which meant I ate mine in a smelly toilet cubicle. It was this empowering interaction at the beginning of lunch:

Zit-faced kid: 'Hey, are you Mia Mannix?'

Me: 'Who wants to know, Zit Face?'

Zit-faced kid: 'I heard you'll pay $100 for a guy to pop your cherry. I'm in.'

Me: 'No. Freakin'. Way.'

Zit-faced kid (to my retreating back): 'How's next Friday?'

I pounded on the door desperately. No answer. I started again, louder. 'I'm having a crisis!' I yelled. 'Open up!'

Emil unlocked his office door and peered out suspiciously. 'This time, ensure the champagne is cold. Not tepid, not chilling, *cold.*'

I almost knocked him over on my way in. 'Oh man, I've never been so glad to see anyone in my life!' I sunk into the beat-up green sofa with sweet relief. 'I am having the worst day of my entire life.'

'Sissy demanding you fetch her virgin sacrifices?'

'Sissy isn't talking to me at all. Plus I've discovered that smoking dope and downing cocktails makes one feel like cutting one's head off and drowning it in ice water. I'm a notch above coma patient, *seriously.*' I continued to relay my tale of woe as Emil unearthed an ancient kettle to make two cups of peppermint tea. Libby settled happily in my lap, chewing on my bag with her sharp puppy teeth. 'And the worst part is, I've totally blown my chance with Ju——, with every guy there.' I sipped my tea morosely.

Emil settled in next to me. 'Pfft. You don't want those tight-black-jean, hipster boys hanging round, anyway.' He pushed his glasses up his nose with authority. 'Everyone knows tight black jeans turn you to the dark side.'

'Huh?'

'It's all there in *Star Wars*.' His eyes sparkled excitedly. 'Take Luke Skywalker in *Return of the Jedi* — originator of the tight-black-jeans look. So all that stuff has just gone down on Sail Barge: Jabba's dead, the droids have escaped, Han and Lando are free, and Boba Fett is being digested by the Sarlacc, right?'

'Right.' I had NFI what he was on about, but the boy was clearly on a roll.

'Even though he *knows* he's in the clear, Luke turns around and blows Jabba's Sail Barge to smithereens!' He laughed in disbelief. 'I mean, the Barge was packed with alien wastoids just trying to have a good time after a hard day in the Galaxy. Rough and ugly? Yes. Evil? No. That's *exactly* the kind of cold-blooded action Obi-Wan warned Luke about. The dark side, kid — the dark *jeans* side.' He slapped his knee triumphantly, turning towards me in expectation.

Confession time. 'I haven't actually seen *Star Wars*.'

'What?' Emil's voice went pre-pubescent with surprise, before his face slowly changed to a look of horror. 'You must think I'm the biggest nerd in the world right about now.'

'I'm sure it was a really good analogy,' I offered helpfully.

'I, um, have some deadlines to make today, Mia.' He was turning the colour of beetroot dip. 'You better go.'

'You can't send me back out there!' I stuttered. 'Wait, tell me more about *Star Wars*! Who's Luke Skyrunner? Is that Harrison Ford?'

I left Emil's office feeling worse than when I went in. Staggeringly Superficial Nikki was right: I was the most pathetic person in the history of the world. *Here Lies Mia Mannix,* my gravestone would read, *A Pash-Virgin Without A Tan.* Or maybe, *The Daughter of Some Famous Guy Who Never Accomplished Anything Herself.* No wait, *The Girl Who Didn't Know About* Star Wars *Or Channing Tatum Because She Was A Massive Loser.* People wouldn't mourn at my grave, they'd laugh at it. No, they wouldn't just laugh at it, they'd . . . woah! My self-deprecating reverie was so consuming that I'd almost run headlong into the Star Sisters themselves, striding up the corridor. Freaked, I side-stepped into an empty music classroom. They passed me unseen, high school royalty complete with an entourage of enraptured students in their wake.

'And then I was like, Mia, we don't care if you think you're too weird and creepy to get a guy, we just wanna be your friend.' Sissy had her 'caring' tone on.

'But she was all crazy-like and yelling. "I'm too ugly! I'll die a virgin!"' Nikki waved her hands around for emphasis.

'And then she ran at us . . . with a knife!' Stacey nodded furiously at the gasps from the kids around her, voices fading as they rounded the corner. 'I think it was a hunting knife – and it had *blood* on it . . .'

'Perfect,' I said to myself. 'Now I'm not just an ugly virgin, I'm also a serial killer.'

'Could you spare me?'

I whirled around with a squeak. A handsome preppy boy was fixing his tie in the reflection of a tuba. 'This shirt cost me two hundred dollars.'

'And in here we'll also find the string instruments. In order for a string instrument to produce sound, its strings must vibrate. You can achieve this by plucking, bowing or striking.' The boy – Seb – paused for effect. 'I prefer striking, because it also describes my ethnic good looks.'

I giggled. 'Italiano?'

He feigned outrage. 'Greek, baby. Hey, we only invented culture, philosophy and the most delicious desserts known to humankind.'

'I didn't even know we had an instrument storeroom.' I followed him, curious. 'You mean, everyone has access to this?'

'Just us music students,' he replied, as he swiped his student card in the lock. 'Come on in.'

I couldn't help but gasp as the door swung open. It was a treasure-trove, teaming with beautifully kept musical instruments of all shapes and sizes. The soft light made everything gleam gently, like something out of a dream. I shivered, giddy, letting the instruments' energy flow up through my fingers and toes. It smelt like orange-oil wood polish and felt magical.

'Wow,' I murmured, mesmerised. 'This place is incredible!' Turning up an aisle, I saw something that stopped me in my tracks. Words stuck in my throat and my mouth fell open, breath shortening, pulse starting a running race. 'Omigod, that's a Rickenbacker 360/12!'

Reaching out carefully, as though it was a wild animal that might take flight, I let my fingers slide gently down the guitar's fretboard, stunned. 'I've only ever seen these in magazines — they cost thousands of dollars! This is, like, the best guitar in the whole world!'

'For a Vis Arts student, you seem pretty down with stuff that makes sound.' Seb furrowed his eyebrows at me. 'Do you play?'

Dad's face floated before me. I had made a deal. 'I used to.' I let my hands slip from the Rickenbacker. 'But art's my thing now.' Time for a change of subject. 'So, pray tell, what's a well-spoken musical genius like yourself doing spending our glorious lunchbreak locked away in the music department?'

He arched an eyebrow. 'I could ask you the same question, Mia.'

I ran my fingers over the strings of a violin, making thin, alien music. 'Removing myself from the less-pleasant elements of high school life.'

'Then we must be kindred spirits.' We exchanged a look of understanding as the end-of-lunch bell rang. We wrinkled our noses and groaned.

'Back to the toil and trouble,' I sighed.

'Fire burn and cauldron bubble ... Good luck escaping the witches three this arvo.'

'Thanks.' I slung my bag over my shoulder. 'Hey — um ...'

'What?'

'Oh, never mind . . .'

'My bat-senses are telling me you have a question. Allow the magic 8-ball to answer for me.'

'You carry an 8-ball around?' I laughed. 'That's so cool!'

'It never lies,' he intoned, shaking the black-and-white fortune-teller gently. 'Ask away.'

'O magic 8-ball,' I began dramatically. 'Will Seb meet me after school for a lemon gelato.'

Seb smiled, and we watched the answer settle: 'My sources say no.'

'Ah screw the 8-ball.' It fell back into his bag with a thud. 'I'll meet you out front.'

Maths and Science passed in a boring blur of fractals and bubbling beakers. Care factor zero on the the kids who kept quoting *Crocodile Dundee* ('That's not a knife. *This* is a knife!') whenever I passed them. I had a friend date! A frate! With someone who was cool and funny and knew about music! Maybe I'd scored a sitcom happy ending to my second day after all . . .

'Darling, it's been too long.' Seb broke his slouchy, model pose against the school fence to air kiss me on both cheeks. Someone happy to see me? I must've stumbled into another dimension. Around us kids spilled into the bright afternoon in a blur of scooters and sunglasses. The sun was shining. I'm pretty sure that, beneath the low roar of traffic, there may have been birds singing. I sighed contentedly, letting the tension of the day melt away like . . . well, like:

'Gelato?'

'I thought you'd never ask.'

We turned in the direction of iced delights . . . and then someone shot me.

Bang!

Suddenly I wasn't standing, I was on the ground, the wind knocked out of me

Bang!

Was I bleeding? Seb was on the ground next to me and we were . . . wet.

Bang!

Kids were pointing and screaming. No . . . wait . . . they were . . . laughing.

'C'mon!' Seb grabbed my hand and pulled me up as another water balloon hit me, finally drenching us completely. All eyes were on us: helpless, drowned rats.

'Oh, would you look at that – you're all wet.' The Star Sisters were suddenly in front of us, Nikki snapping a picture on her iPhone. I snatched at it but she was too quick, and she grabbed my arm tightly.

Her tone was low and menacing in my ear. 'Play with fire, and you will get burned.' Then, with a curt toss of her head, 'Let's go, girls.'

The witches sashayed off, leaving my potential new friend and me looking like the victims of a small, isolated rainstorm, to the delight of the school population's camera phones.

'Do you have a car?' I asked desperately. 'We gotta get out of the public eye *asap*.'

'I get the bus,' Seb coughed awkwardly. 'And BTW . . . your shirt is kinda . . . see-through.'

'Oh no,' I moaned, crossing my arms. 'What are we gonna do?'

From out of nowhere, a beat-up red Cadillac pumping screamy punk-rock pulled up, tyres screeching in front of the school. The passenger door was flung open. Behind the wheel, in a smoky haze, sat Lexie. Seb and I swapped a bewildered glance.

'You waiting for a printed invite?' she snapped. 'Get in!'

Soundtrack: 'Kapow!', Young and Restless
Mood: Scared, wet, in a car

A few years ago a photographer from some glossy art mag came round to our house to take snaps of Dad painting and making cups of tea and pass them off as photo-journalism. His name was Dan Danielson, a vaguely sleazy dude who looked like a rabbit with a pencil moustache. He took photos of me reading *Rolling Stone*, insisting I 'forget he was there'. Considering he stank of garlic and B.O., that proved impossible. I remember feeling super awkward — but that memory pales in comparison to being squished in between a wet Seb and a cold Lexie. In this chick's book, orange meant hit the gas not the brakes. Overtaking? As mandatory as simultaneously lighting cigarettes, fiddling with the radio and blasting the horn at drivers who got in your way. Out of the frying pan and into a speed-limit-free fire . . . I was on edge, and completely petrified.

'Thanks so much for the ride,' began Seb, shouting over the music. 'I'm Seb . . .'

'I didn't do it for you, Seth.' Lexie slammed on the brakes at a red light and we were all thrown forward. My heart stopped, realised I was still alive, and kept beating.

'I'm sorry, what? And ah, it's Seb.'

'I didn't do it for you.' The CD ended, leaving the car in stilted silence. 'I didn't want to give the Bimbo Brigade the satisfaction.' For emphasis, she flicked her cigarette butt hard out the window.

We watched it arc towards a chi-chi outdoor restaurant, landing smack-bang in a plate of pasta. A wrinkly, beehive-haired woman jumped in fright at the unwanted garnish, instinctively sweeping the plate onto the ground, which crashed straight in a burningly efficient waiter's path.

I squeaked in a combination of fright and delight, as the guy stumbled and spilt two bowls of bright red soup all over himself. Everyone's heads jerked like puppets on a string as they looked for the culprit.

'Green, green!' Seb spluttered, flapping his hands at the lights.

The woman and the waiter started running at the car, faces screwed up in anger.

'Drive! Quick!' I yelled, adrenaline pumping. 'Lexie, go!!'

She shrieked, one purple-heeled foot slamming down the accelerator, popping us forward like a bullet from a gun. We zoomed off, all of us screaming with laughter.

Topics like 'going home' and 'hey, weren't you totally mean to me the other day?' seemed off-limits, so instead we bought hot chips and cruised around town, channel-surfing the radio and bonding through bitching about the one thing we had in common.

'They're so lame,' Lexie groaned. 'Shopping with them is like, "Do you like this dress? I don't know, do you like it? I like it if she likes it.". Gag times a trillion.'

'You used to hang with them?' I licked salt off my fingers, half-fascinated, half-scared of the tempestuous blonde.

'Kinda.' We swung viciously into a service station. 'I gotta fill up.'

A couple of old dudes in trucker caps and flannies stared as Lexie made a show of suggestively pumping petrol. Seb leaned forward. 'She used to *be* a Star Sister.'

'*What*?' I choked on a chip. 'What happened?'

He shrugged. 'She was in the band last year, when she was this massively goody-two-shoes Head Girl. Then her parents divorced and she – ah – changed.' Despite the fact that she was well out of earshot, Seb's voice dropped to a whisper. 'Apparently, she got busted at the end of last year for showing up to this really important school presentation not exactly sober, and calling the Prime Minister a dickhead. Word is a substantial donation to the school was the only reason she wasn't expelled.'

I was beyond stunned as I watched her wait in line with toe-tapping impatience, totally punk in a ripped Blondie singlet and gold football shorts, roughed up and raw. Flaxen blonde hair fell in knots, nail polish chipped.

'She's a fallen angel,' ancient knowledge flooded my

imagination, 'banished from the heavens for rebelling against God.'

Seb nodded as Lexie tossed a twenty over like it was trash. 'Doomed to walk the Earth 'til Judgement Day.'

The angel in question grabbed a handful of chocolate bars as she accepted her change, daring the pimply sales guy to do anything about it as she turned and strutted out.

'Did you see that?' Disbelief reigned. 'She didn't pay for those, she just took them, and the guy let her walk right out!'

'Would you have the guts to stop someone like that?' Seb asked, as Lexie strode back to the car.

'Dessert.' She chucked a bar at us both, before revving the engine. 'I've got a surprise for you guys.'

'It's like a car crash in slow motion,' Seb decided. 'Less "Girls Gone Wild", more "Girls in Need of Serious Medical Attention".' He shifted onto his side to face us. 'Scenario: You've just woken up from a ten-year coma. The doc instructs you to pole dance.' Hands flourished in the Star Sisters' direction. 'Result.'

Lexie laughed loudly. 'You're hilarious! Swift me!'

Seb high-fived her, only slightly confused.

'Gimme those!' I snatched the binoculars from Seb and trained them on the dance studio across the street from the park we were lying in. In it, Sissy and Stacey were teaching Nikki the art of the body roll. Well, that's what they thought they were doing . . .

'Impersonating a caterpillar? A very, very sick caterpillar?' I chewed a blade of grass as three asses shook in formation, before one lost the rhythm. 'It's ironic, isn't it — women burnt their bras so these girls can dance around in theirs.'

Lexie snorted. 'I can't believe they boned Gillian for Nikki — she's not even a real dancer.'

Seb brushed some stray dirt from his sleeve. 'I thought Nikki was a sports nerd.'

'She was when I knew her.' Lexie cracked her knuckles.

I glanced at her, feigning casual disinterest. 'So, what's the story there?'

'Whaddya talking about?' Her tone walked the line between innocence and insolence.

'Your dalliance with the dark side. Former friendship with the witches three.'

Her expression was inscrutable beneath the shiny black sunglasses that clung to her face like space-age armour. 'People change'.

Who first — her or them? Why? How? I decided not to push it — for now — and rolled onto my back to address the sky. 'When I moved here I thought there'd be a million cool bands playing in dark little cafes and falling-down warehouses, all underground and over everyone's heads. Singers who scowl and spit, not these plastic Barbie girls. I mean, that's not even the point of music!'

'I have total girl crush on Karen O — the chick in the Yeah Yeah Yeahs,' Lexie shook her hair out, energised. 'She doesn't care what anyone thinks! She's like a wild animal onstage!'

'Exactly!' I exclaimed. 'She's real and raw, and their songs are *awesome*.'

'From a technical point of view, the Star Sisters' beats are cut-price cheap.' Seb frowned as the cheesy pop track floated past us on the breeze. 'Anyone could do better than that. *I* could.'

'Really?' I glanced at him, eyebrows on high.

'I dabble.'

Lexie's gold shorts caught the light, glowing like a forest fire as she lit a cigarette. Seb sat back on his elbows, inspecting his cuticles with a frown. An idea was unfolding inside me. 'Hey. You know what we look like?'

'Freaks,' Lexie muttered.

'Geeks,' countered Seb.

'*A band.*'

Our heads turned like tennis coaches as we regarded each other, mentally making a whole.

'I'd love to be in a band. A real band,' Lexie grinned. 'Revenge rock. Give those three a run for their money.'

'Cool idea,' Seb shrugged. 'But you guys don't play an instrument.' He glanced at me deliberately. 'Right, Mia?'

Defeated, I let my gaze drop to the grass in front of me, quickly back on earth.

'That's right,' I replied woodenly. 'I don't play an instrument. No instrument playing for me.'

'You guys, what is going on here?' Lex demanded. 'Did you drop acid behind my back?'

'She's like, some kind of guitar genius, but her dad banned her,' Seb started informing Lexie matter-of-factly.

'I'm not!' I interrupted. 'I can't . . .'

'*Can't* play guitar, or not *allowed* to play guitar?' Lex asked, suddenly in top lawyer mode.

'Not allowed,' I replied meekly. 'Seriously, a band is actually a bad idea right now . . .'

'She can play guitar!' Lex screeched, pummelling Seb with excitement. 'We can really do this! I can sing . . .'

'You're looking at a drum machine that walks and talks,' quipped Seb. 'Boom-tish!'

'Forget pop princesses, dumb dance moves and the plastic fantastic,' Lexie spat. 'I'm so in! *We can start a band!*'

'Guys, no, we can't.' I summoned every ounce of authority I had in me. 'I made a deal with my dad. He agreed to move to Sydney if I focused on art class and quit "wasting time" with my hobbies. I can't break my promise.'

A silenced Seb and Lexie exchanged glances, clearly stuffed with a thousand strategies. It was Seb who stepped up to the task first. 'Mia, I saw you in the instrument storeroom,' he began. 'Can you honestly tell me music is just a "hobby" for you?'

Oh man, what am I getting myself into? 'But, I promised . . .'

'So what, I break promises all the time!' grinned Lex. 'Situations change. You didn't know you could start a band when you made that promise. You want to, right?'

'Yeah,' I admitted.

'And you're still gonna go to art classes, right?' Seb continued.

'Obviously . . .'

'Plus, you'd get to borrow the Rickenbacker . . .'

'I *would*?' The prospect made me feel tingly, as though there were sparks shooting spitfire around my head.

'So follow your heart. How hard is that?' They both bug-eyed me.

Thoughts tumbled through my head like rain. They were right. Music wasn't just a hobby. I'd *only* made that deal to escape the concentration camp of country living. I'd never broken a promise to Dad before . . . but this felt *right*. This felt like what I was supposed to do. How can you argue with fate?

'Okay.' Adrenaline rushed like a double-latte overload. 'Let's do it.'

Their whooping sent magpies ducking for cover.

Then Seb was up, pulling us to our feet. 'Let's fight fire with fire. Now all we need is a name.'

It came to me in a flash. 'Fire Fire.'

And just like that, it was decided.

Soundtrack: 'Pixelated', Terrapin

Mood: Happy and enthusiastic about something that is happening or is about to happen

We sped to mine for a change of clothes and supplies, electricity coursing through us and the radio up full bore.

'We're *rock stars*,' hooted Lexie, overtaking soccer mums in a frenzy of burnt rubber and speed-cameras-be-damned.

'I'm sure that'll hold up in court,' I thought, checking for the umpteenth time that my seatbelt was firmly fastened.

Demo CDs for the Battle of the Bands competition had been due by the end of the day, but in our newly aligned state we'd quickly devised a plan. Using Seb's student card we would sneak into the school's recording studio after dark and pull an all-nighter: jam up a melody, pen some lyrics, and record a song in time to sneak it into the entry box before school began in the early a.m. We were a band with a plan.

'Nice digs.' Seb let out a low whistle as we pulled up to my pad.

I snuck a look at Lexie, unsure. 'You don't have to come in, if you don't wanna . . .'

'Are you kidding?' She grinned impishly. 'How can I be mean about your wardrobe in the car?' It was as close to an apology as I was ever gonna get.

'You know, there's more to being in a band than angular haircuts and cool clothes,' Seb said, as we crunched up the driveway together. 'And I'm sure eventually we'll work out what that is. But for now, I see afterparties.' He touched his temples, fortune teller-like. 'Crowds of people wearing sunglasses at night . . .'

'Drag queens and deros,' Lexie continued, as I opened the door.

'Saints and sinners,' I announced to the empty house. 'Cool cats and Cosmos!'

Seb stuck me in the ribs, his voice low in my ear. 'Don't look now but there's a high school cleaner in the lounge room. And he looks, well, angry.'

I turned weakly. 'Hi, Dad.'

Dad's discipline technique was usually the 'I'm not mad, I'm just disappointed' mantra. It worked. Every time. When he found cigarettes in a shoebox under my bed, he simply sighed and commented that he thought I was 'smarter than that'. I felt dumb, flushed the cigs down the toilet, and haven't touched one since. But right now, he was just mad.

'Mia, we need to talk.' His glasses slipped down his nose as he ran a hand through his curly, unkempt hair.

I shifted, embarrassed. 'Dad, I have *friends* here.' Who were making a poor attempt at pretending to admire the harbour views, eavesdropping with barely concealed fascination.

'Your friends will have to wait. *This* requires an explanation.' A tabloid newspaper hit the kitchen bench.

'Oh, Dad,' I sighed, scanning the white-teethed babes smiling blankly, momentarily stunned by the photographer's flash. 'Don't freak out, but it's called a "social section", and yes, it is indicative of the decay of contemporary culture and . . . oh please no, "Playboy Sal Mannix makes a move."'

I snatched up the paper, recognising *that* photo of Dad with his arm round a laughing Radha Mitchell, reading in

53

horror: Reclusive artist Sal Mannix joins the A-list this week, taking up residence in fashionable Somerset Drive — and he's already got his eye on a number of local lasses! Mia Mannix, 15, only daughter of the famous painter, says her dad is in town looking for love . . . . *What!?*

Dad's eyes were thunderous. I continued painfully. Mia told classmates at the prestigious Silver Street Performing Arts High School that her famous father was 'into' Penny King, real estate agent to the stars, describing her as 'a total babe'. Mrs King stated she was 'flattered', but would have to consult with her husband before accepting any dinner offers.

The paper dropped from my fingers. My stomach churned, seasick.

'And then, there's this.' Dad's voice was dangerously calm as he slid towards me an empty envelope with *Cherry* scrawled across it in my handwriting. 'When I found this in the bin, I figured you must have started buying your school supplies — until I found these in your room.'

The designer dress, handbag and shoes I'd bought in a last-minute shopping frenzy for the twins' party sat innocently on the end of the kitchen counter.

'Cute heels.' Lexie reached for them in kid-sees-candy mode, before being tugged back by Seb.

'We'll, uh, wait in your room. Upstairs, right?' He shot me a *you're screwed* look as he shepherded Lexie away. Tell me something I don't know.

'Gossip columns? Expensive clothes?' Dad stared at me, completely disorientated. 'Mia, what is going on?'

'I can explain,' I said firmly, with absolutely no explanation in mind.

He nodded, averting his eyes. 'Yes, well, you'll have plenty of time for that because you're . . . you're grounded until you can replace that money.'

'What? No!' My eyes flicked up to see Lexie and Seb staring at me from the top of the staircase, shaking their heads vehemently. (Well, Seb was looking at me. I think Lexie was still looking at the shoes.) 'You can't ground me, we're starting a band!'

'A band?' Dad took 'incredulous' to a whole new level. Wrong move, girl!

'A band . . . of study buddies. It's what they call it here.' I shrugged, smiling winningly. 'And I really can explain. Let's, ah, sit outside.'

Unseen mozzies buzzed round our bare arms in the twilight air, still thick with humidity and sticky salt. Dad sat opposite me, glaring like a cop at a crim who won't 'fess up. Okay, Mannix, I steeled myself. One chance only. Don't screw up.

'I took the money for those clothes because I was invited to a party and I didn't have anything to wear. Literally! My clothes were all in transit. And I said that stuff in class because, well, I wanted the kids to like me. I didn't know it'd end up in the paper.'

'You don't have to tell stories and buy clothes to make friends, Mia,' he tutted.

'Yeah, I know,' I exhaled. 'It was a mistake. I'm really sorry.'

'And as for a party being a priority . . .'

'It was a one-off! A back-to-school thing for our year. You want me to make friends, right? Well, I made some, but if you ground me I can't go to the study buddy . . . band sleepover they've invited me to.'

He frowned. 'I can see your new friends look very trendy, Mia . . .'

'Don't say *trendy*.'

'Groovy?'

'Just stay away from adjectives altogether.'

He cracked a smile before 'serious Dad' took over again.

'I know you can't appreciate this now, but you need to take your education seriously.' Uh oh, attack of the parental clichés. Time to look serious and nod. 'I know you'll be faced with a lot of distractions this year, like new friends and boys, I suppose, and . . .'

Boys. With all the excitement of starting the hottest new band in the world, I'd completely forgotten about my Number One Untouchable Crush: Justin. Justin, who's in a band. A band like me! Scenarios swarmed:

I've finished up a long night of rehearsal at Shaky's, guitar case in hand and looking supercute, waving my two kewl bandmates goodbye. He notices me, surprised. 'Mia — I didn't know you played guitar. Can I drive you home?' Or maybe: 'Hey Mia, *everyone's* talking about Fire Fire. Wanna come back to my place for a swim?' 'But Justin, I haven't got any swimmers.' 'That's cool babe, we don't *need* swimmers . . .'

'I said . . . wouldn't you agree?' Dad's voice finished my fantasies.

'Sh'yeah, of course!' I exclaimed.

Apparently that had been the right thing to say. 'All right then. I'll cover the seven hundred and fifty dollars as a back-to-school gift, *and* you can go to your study sleepover tonight . . .'

'Thanks, Dad!'

'*If*, Mia, *if* that's the first and *last* time this sort of thing happens.' Dad took my hand and looked me square in the eye. 'You have so much natural talent as a painter, honey. Now that we've moved here, like you wanted, I do not want you to throw that away.'

I squeezed his hand hard. 'Don't worry. This year I'm going to be one hundred per cent devoted to my art. I *promise*.'

Dad nodded in relief as I brushed away the niggles of guilt. Music's art, right?

Soundtrack: 'Down Down Down', The Presets
Mood: Thrillseeking

To most people, schools only exist in the bright light of day, flooded with stampeding feet and waves of noisy chatter. At night it was a different story: a spooky, strange setting for a low-budget horror. We were turning the natural order of the world on its head, skulking through shadows with the silent determination of jewel thieves. As we passed my English classroom, lines from *Hamlet* drifted back to me, *There are more things in heaven and earth, Horatio, than are dreamt of in your philosophy* . . . We were discovering them.

Pools of moonlight turned our faces ghostly pale as Seb swiped his card outside the Music Department. He flicked on the lights and a thrill ran right through me. On one side of the room, several computers lay dormant, plugged into all manner of speakers and mixing decks. Wires everywhere. On the other side, behind a glass window, was a single microphone – the recording studio. Seb began switching on machines, their lights blinking as they whirred to life.

'How do we wanna do this?' he asked.

'How about, you do all the work and I'll get all the credit.' Lexie grinned at our shocked faces. 'You guys, I'm *kidding*.'

Seb smiled wryly. 'I was thinking more along the lines of: we brainstorm some general ideas of what we want to sound like, then I'll set up a drum kit and keyboard, and me and Mia can start jamming and laying some stuff down.'

'While I write a kickass song.' Lexie raised her fists in a rock salute. 'Thank you! Good night!'

'You can work in the instrument storeroom – get inspired by oboes. But first,' Seb produced a leather-bound notebook, pen poised above a blank sheet, 'throw some words at me.'

'Sexy.' No prizes for guessing whose mind that had sprung to.

'*Sexy.*' Seb scribbled it down.

'Cool,' Lexie continued. 'But hot.'

'Hot *and* cool,' mused Seb. 'A meteorological musical conundrum. Mia?'

They both looked at me and suddenly, weirdly, I clammed up. Seb knew what he was doing with all those computers and mixers and microphones, and Lexie could speak her mind like she'd been born with people asking her opinion ('Shall we cut the cord now or later?'). I loved playing the guitar, but I didn't know anything about being in a band. I was a fraud.

'Um, I don't know . . .' I stared at my shoes.

'C'mon,' Seb frowned. 'Don't tell me the button badge girl doesn't have some good ideas. You're the one who got us here in the first place.'

'Can't you guys can work this stuff out?' I mumbled.

'No way.' Lexie stuck her hands on her hips, defiant. 'If we're gonna do this, everyone has to be in. No secrets, no backing out. No *wimping* out.'

'It's just . . . I don't . . . I don't know anything about – well – anything.' I waved my hand in the direction of the banks of computers and cables. 'I've never even played in front of anyone else before. I hate public speaking. What if I hate being onstage? I don't think I can do this . . .'

'Woah! Easy with the mental breakdown, Mannix,' Seb interrupted. 'We're not selling out stadiums just yet. Why don't you just describe what you'd like Fire Fire to be like. Positive visualisation.'

'Okay,' I breathed. 'But this will probably sound lame.' I closed my eyes, letting myself imagine. 'All right . . . so we're playing in some back-alley club. It's smoky and the stage is small. Seb's pounding the drums rhythmically and the synth sounds like spooky, sexy disco — not rock, more electro. My guitar sounds choppy — dark, unrelenting. A crowd of kids are dancing, 'cause it's got a beat: pop but dangerous. Lexie's writhing onstage like a serpent, spitting lyrics about death to dumb boys, wild stories, building the crowd up. Unpredictable and scary-cool. Music for rock'n'roll vampires.'

I opened my eyes. Lexie and Seb were both staring at me in fascination. Seb cleared his throat. 'Right. Well, that sounds . . .'

'Totally. Freakin'. *Hot*.' Lexie twirled in excitement. 'If I wasn't totally hetero I'd make out with you right now!'

I laughed in surprise. 'I guess that's good.'

Lexie grabbed Seb's notebook. 'Guys, get to work. I've got a song to write.'

'Meet back here at 0100 hours!' called Seb as the whirlwind slammed the door. 'Right.' He turned his attention to me, a wicked gleam in his eyes. 'So. Are you ready to rock?'

Three hours, several false starts, several more musical breakthroughs, one pizza and three vending machine coffees later, it was a very happy Mia Mannix who bounced up to check on our songstress.

'It's going great,' I began excitedly before she even asked. 'Everything's totally coming together. At first I was a bit clunky, 'cause I've never played with drums before, but Seb is so cool to work with, and playing the Rickenbacker is incredible, it practically plays for you. And after our third coffee we started having all these amazing ideas, and the guitar part and the drums are pretty much done, so now Seb's messing round on the keys and we need you to come in and try some lyric ideas out, and show us what you've written . . .'

'That all sounds peachy, Mia,' Lex snapped. 'But there is no song.' She threw the notebook down. It was blank. It was past one a.m. and she hadn't even written one word.

I drew in a shaky breath, trying to get my head around how to make this work. 'Okay . . . well, I guess that's because you haven't heard the music yet. That's fair enough. Maybe we should go back to the studio and——'

'And what? I'll hear the "awesome" stuff you guys have done, open my mouth and sing a whole finished song? I don't think so!'

I sat down opposite her. 'What do you want me to do?'

She rolled her eyes, and I glimpsed the cracks in the tough-girl mask. 'I dunno. Help me.'

'All right.' I picked up the notebook gingerly. 'Let's start with a theme. What about . . . love.'

'Love sucks.' Lexie's eyes darkened. 'I hate love.'

I wrote that down. 'What else?'

'I dunno.' She blew hair out of her eyes like a snorting horse. 'Boys suck. They lie and they're mean.'

I printed the words carefully and looked back up. 'Can you give me examples?'

'No!' She threw me an annoyed look. 'This is beyond pointless. Plus, it's personal.'

'You said no secrets. Do you want my help or not?'

'Fine,' she said grudgingly, crossing her arms. 'What other *private things* do you want to know?'

The gruff voice of an old journalist who'd once interviewed Dad floated back to me: *Ask the tough questions kid,* he'd belched, pudgy fingers wrapped round a sweaty tin of VB. *Even if they don't answer, they'll respect you for trying.*

'Why did you do . . . *that* with Sissy's boyfriend?'

Lexie's mouth fell open, a storm whipped up behind baby-blue eyes, baiting me. 'Do what?'

'You know. Hook up.' I returned her gaze calmly, bracing myself for a torrent of abuse.

Instead she just breathed out with deliberate calm, fixing her gaze to a point on the floor. 'Sissy was away. Stuff just happens.'

'But wasn't she your friend . . .'

Lexie's laugh was hard. 'She'd have done the same thing to me. Plus, I was doing her a favour. You can't trust guys.' Her voice rose. 'At the end of the day, they're all liars and they're all cheats! I never wanna be with a guy again!'

She picked up the nearest thing – the notebook – and threw it across the room, trembling. Slowly, I reached for her hand, and she let me fold my fingers into hers.

'That's good, 'cause you won't have time for a boyfriend now. You're in the coolest band in the whole world. Everything's changing.'

She looked back at me, a smile spreading across her face.

'What?' I asked, involuntarily starting to smile too. 'What!?'

She grabbed the notepad confidently. 'You want a song about love? Gimme twenty minutes.'

'Guys, it's five a.m.!' Lexie groaned from behind the glass. 'Do I have to do it again?'

'Just one more chorus!'

She slipped the headphones back on and Seb hit play on the backing track. Catchy, minimal electro-punk beats filled the studio, and Lexie closed her eyes, letting it wash over her, moving in time to the music. Despite our exhaustion, the effect was mesmerising.

Seb spoke through the studio intercom. 'Okay, here it comes.' The chorus kicked in and Lexie began to sing, her raspy voice dripping with equal parts sex and sarcasm — effortless attitude bleeding through the speakers.

He's gonna ch-ch-change,
I know the k-k-kind.
I'm not gonna waste,
Any of my t-t-time.
I said, She's gonna ch-ch-change,
Yeah, I know the k-k-kind . . .

Seb shook away a yawn. 'For a first song, I reckon it's pretty good. Your guitar stuff sounds great.'

I flushed with pride as Lexie pirouetted back into the room.

'So. We're done, right?' she asked.

'Nearly.' Seb slid over to another computer and switched it on. 'I just have to record the synth melodies then mix everything back. It'll only take a couple of hours. Don't worry,' he laughed at our stricken faces. 'You guys can rest till I'm done.'

'I wanna learn, Seb,' I yawned. 'I really do . . . I'll just close my eyes for a few minutes and then you can show me . . .'

I gasped, my eyes flying open. Sunlight streamed through the windows. Over the ringing of the school bell, muffled footsteps and laughter filtered under the door. Lexie lay sprawled on the floor, head thrown back and snoring softly. Seb was peacefully passed out in his chair by the computer. Sitting up groggily I checked my phone for the time. Nine a.m. Huh? *Nine a.m.?*

Two minutes later we were sprinting towards the front office, clothes crumpled, hair an early-morning mess.

'Coming through!' Lexie yelled, brandishing our demo like a relay runner's baton. 'Move it or lose it!'

Racing up to the office we barrelled around the corner and straight into: 'Mrs Prisk!' We panted in relief. 'We made it!'

She glared at us through hawk-like eyes. 'If that's a Battle of the Bands entry, you're too late.'

'What?' we spluttered. 'But . . .'

'No buts.' Her voice cut like a knife. 'The deadline was *yesterday*. You children have no *discipline*.'

Shooting us one final death-stare, she turned and strode off with all the precision of an army major, leaving us help-lessly staring after her. Lexie kicked a stone and swore.

Seb went pale, staring at the disc in his hand. 'But . . . we worked so hard,' he said limply.

I slumped down against the wall in shock. 'I was so sure we'd be in that competition . . .'

'Hey.'

I looked up to see Emil wheeling his bike in through the school gates.

'Welcome to the Loser Club,' I muttered, 'where all your dreams turn to dust.' I nodded at the rapidly disappearing figure of Prisk-the-Witch. 'We made an entry for Battle of the Bands. But there goes our chance to enter it . . .'

Emil reached out and plucked the CD from Seb's fingers.

'Hey, that's our . . .' Seb started in confusion.

Emil jumped on his bike and sped in the direction of Prisk. Confused, we ran after him.

'Mrs Prisk! Wait!' Emil yelled, rounding the corner as she headed to her car. We hid behind some bushes and watched. 'Mrs Prisk, I'm the editor of the school paper and I was wondering if I could interview you for – whoops!'

Bam! He cycled straight into her. The box of CDs flew out of her hands, spilling everywhere.

'Oh, you silly boy!'

'I'm sorry, Ma'am.' On his hands and knees, Emil was scooping up the CDs. We nudged each other in disbelief. He had just mixed up our demo with the ones on the ground . . .

'I don't have time for your silly paper now,' she snapped, snatching the box from him. 'Get to class before I report you!'

As she drove off, Emil turned to give us a thumbs-up.

Lexie ran over and threw herself on him, squealing happily. 'I don't know who you are but *you rock*!' she yelled, smacking a kiss loudly on each of his cheeks.

Seb shook Emil's hand enthusiastically. 'Cool. Very cool.'

'Thanks, Emil.' I squeezed his arm, and he glanced at me in curiosity.

'You have a knack for trouble, don't you, Miss Mia?'

'Oh, it's part of my charm,' I replied breezily.

He grinned, as we all turned to head back into school. 'Three days in town and you've already made friends, then mortal enemies of the I-can't-believe-they-call-themselves-a-band Star Sisters . . .'

'Been quoted in the paper,' Seb added, 'and attacked by water bombs.'

'Been busted blowing your life savings on clothes and shoes,' Lexie laughed, skipping ahead.

'And now you've started a band,' Emil regarded me with a smile. 'I have a feeling this year's gonna be pretty interesting.'

I couldn't help but think he was right.

Soundtrack: 'Mr Ice Cream', Soft Tigers
Mood: Kickin' it, summer style

January slipped into February and Lexie, Seb and I became a three-for-one deal. At lunchtime we'd meet at the back of the oval to munch on homemade Greek biscuits and work on songs. Lexie would snarl at the boys who let their eyes linger over her long golden legs, and we'd write about things we knew and things we dreamed of.

After school we'd get lost wandering backstreets in search of inspiration and ice-cream, or pile Lexie's car with equipment sneaked out from school (courtesy of Seb's magic music-student card) and rehearse till late at Shaky's. I'd seen Justin there two heart-stopping times, but on both occasions he was busy loading gear into a van and I didn't have the guts to fake a casually surprised hello. In due course, I told myself, ignoring the chicken noises some irritating internal voice kept making.

Dad was always absent, working on new paintings that were due for some exhibition in New York or Hong Kong or London, which made it easy to avoid doing my art homework.

Lexie and Seb would lie to their parents about study sleepovers, we'd order pizza, watch *Rage* and swap stories. I played them songs by bands I was discovering on MySpace: hot angsty boys and dreamy girls with shaggy haircuts singing about mystery and poetry and hidden lives.

Seb began teaching Lexie to play the keyboard, and I learnt more about recording and mixing. Where I was dedicated, Lex was distracted but we made it work.

A cold war had set in between the Star Sisters and Fire Fire, and I was perfecting the art of seeing but not seeing the breezy brashness of Nikki, Sissy and Stacey as they stalked the school corridors like escaped store mannequins turned evil, spreading wicked rumours we learned to ignore.

Emil became my art class confidante, and began a lunch-time course in the World's Most Awesome Movies. When the break was washed out by tropical summer storms we'd stock up on microwave popcorn and pineapple juice, and work our way through wild and wonderful sci-fi classics: *Blade Runner, A Clockwork Orange, Dark City* and more. On the weekends he and I would walk Libby, and after several intensive lessons, I taught her to roll over and shake hands.

School took a backseat. Life was taking over. But there was strangeness during those days too.

Lexie's was often late or AWOL at rehearsal, which usually meant I began discussing my default monologue with Seb — a rather detailed speech about Justin and the various ways he made my brain and body feel. But when I pushed him to dish on his crush, he would get weird and flustered and make an excuse to leave, disappearing to a home we were never invited to.

When I told Lexie about Seb's strange behaviour — me strumming what I now claimed as *my* Rickenbacker, her flicking through a magazine, painting her fingernails Dead-Baby Blue — she raised her eyebrows at me pointedly.

'What?' My fingers strolled up the strings as I faked a French accent. '*Quelle problem?*'

'He bailed when you started talking about another guy?'

'Is there an echo in here? That's what I just said.'

Lexie snorted. 'Join the dots, Mannix.' She flipped through the mag and cleared her throat. '*Mate or Date*,' she read out smugly. '*Is your guy friend really your next boyfriend?*'

'Oh, c'mon Lex,' I snorted. 'This is Seb we're talking about!'

'Let's do the quiz anyway.' She sat up excitedly. Lexie loved multiple choice. '*It's Saturday night. What's your buddy up to? A. NFI — prolly hanging with the guys. B. There're vague plans for your crew to hit a house party or cruise round town. C. Hanging with you, watching DVDs and scoffing pizza.* That's easy. *C*.'

'Are you doing this quiz or am I?' I tossed a stray shoe at her.

'All right, what answer then?' She called my bluff with delight.

I sighed. 'Okay, *C*. But look, I know what you're trying to make it sound like . . .'

'*The idea of pashing your pal makes you feel: A. Grossed out. B. Vaguely curious. C. Totally excited.*'

'*A*. Grossed out,' I shot back.

'Really?' Lexie crossed her arms.

'Yes.' I retorted.

'You're the lamest liar ever! It's *B*, isn't it?'

'No . . .'

Lexie threw the magazine down and pointed at me accusingly. 'Don't lie to me, Mia! You know how much I hate liars!'

'Okay, okay. *B*. Happy?'

Over the next half hour Lexie got more and more worked up as we discovered I could *C. Tell my guy pretty much everything — it's a no secrets kinda deal*, that I thought his appearance was *A. More or less as good as a guy's is gonna get*, and that *B. Actually we're both single, not that it means anything*'.

Lexie channelled the energy of a lap dog on steriods as she added up my score. 'I knew it!' she screamed. 'You're Secret Soulmates!'

'Gimme that!' Palms sweaty, I scanned the answer.

Wake up girlfriend! There's nothing stopping your mate from becoming your date. Think long and hard about your relationship — are you really just friends? Or is he the one for you? Face the fear next time he's near.

Lex stared at me in frozen-faced excitement.

'All right, I'll think "long and hard" about it,' I parroted to her. 'But you've gotta admit, he's no Justin Jackson. No siree.'

'Mmmm . . .' Lexie grabbed the magazine back and made a show of flipping through it without reading.

'What?'

'Nothing, just, *Mmmm.*' She glanced at me wide-eyed.

'Oh man, you're a worse liar than I am,' I laughed. 'C'mon. 'Fess up!'

She stuttered, sounding caught out. 'I just think Justin is bad news — he's thinks he's all that but . . . You need options . . .'

I clapped my hands in front of her face. 'Lex, what's going on?'

She sighed painfully. 'It sucks I've gotta be the one to tell you this, but . . . Nikki and Justin hooked up last weekend.'

It was four a.m. and I was still no closer to sleep than when I'd managed to push an obsessed Lexie out the door at midnight. After an entire evening of her on my case about how perfect Seb and I would be together, I was totally confused. I didn't feel a Justin Jackson-sized crush, but the more I thought about it, the more it started to make sense. Seb was supercool and a Nice Guy. He could write music and was an impeccable dresser. What was the point of crushing on a guy I'd spent a grand total of twenty minutes talking to (and who was now making time with the poisonous Miss Moretti!) when my perfect guy was right in front of my nose?

I got out of bed and opened my window, speaking to the wide, wise expanse of ocean in front of me. 'I like Seb.' My words disappeared into the warm night air, and suddenly, scarily, it was true.

The woman's breasts were perky but soft — about the size of peaches and of similar texture. My eye travelled over and around the dark muddy pink of her nipple, connecting the few tiny moles that spotted the brown skin — tiny towns on a mystery road map. She reclined, comfortable with her curves, eyes blinking slowly as if in a dream . . . And then she sneezed.

We all groaned.

'I'm sorry, I'm sorry.' The life model got back into position as the class shifted and muttered.

'Her left arm was anywhere but there.' Emil erased his last few pencil lines meticulously. 'If I wasn't staring at a naked woman in the name of art, I'd almost be annoyed.'

'Lemme know if you want me to explain anything, Emil.' Michael leaned forward from his easel. 'It must be a shock to see a real woman's body.'

'Actually, your mum's pretty good with explanations,' Emil shot back, and everyone giggled.

'That's enough, monkeys,' reprimanded Rocho, as the end-of-class bell broke up the banter. 'Don't forget that the deadline is coming up for getting me the details of your work for the end-of-term class exhibition. I need the name of the artist or art movement you're basing your work on, and details of the work itself. You must be *at the exhibition* to pass this term. And no, Michael, you can't have the number of the life model for practise at home.'

'What are you doing for the assignment?' Emil asked as we lined up to stack our easels at the back of the room.

'I haven't even thought about it,' I admitted. 'I have less than zero time at the moment.'

'Sex, drugs, rock'n'roll?'

'You said it, mister. Well, the rock'n'roll part anyway.'

'So, are we attempting the *Alien* versus *Alien 2* debate at lunch?' His eyes flashed behind the black rims of his glasses. 'Or is today the day we answer the question: What is *The Matrix* and why did the sequels suck so badly?'

I hoisted my easel on top of the pile. 'I can't. I have something on with Lex.'

'Oh.'

He looked kinda bummed so I quickly added, 'It's really important girl stuff.' (We were rehashing every conversation I'd had with Seb in the last week and analysing them for indications of his true feelings for me.) 'Actually Emil . . . can I ask your advice about something?'

'Sure.'

'All right,' I began, making sure everyone else had well and truly left the room. 'What would you do if . . . um, no wait,' I exhaled, confused. 'Say you're friends with someone, and you really like being friends with them and then, one day, you think maybe . . . maybe you wanna be more than just friends . . .'

'Okay . . .'

'Would you tell them?' I shifted my weight from one foot to the next, suddenly with ants in my pants. 'And how would you tell them? And what if they don't feel the same way, does that ruin things? And if it does ruin things . . .'

'Wait, stop,' he grinned self-consciously. 'I think I get it.'

'So, what do I do?'

He ran his fingers through his hair, almost shyly. 'You make a move.'

'Really?'

'Yes,' he grinned again. 'Definitely.'

'But what if it turns out they don't like me back?'

'Mia, you're . . . you're smart, and creative and cool and . . . c'mon, you know you're cute,' He stopped himself and shook his head, reddening. 'I know for a fact your friend likes you back.'

'Really? You know Seb likes me?' My mouth dropped open in surprise.

'Seb?'

'Did Lexie tell you to ask him? She did, didn't she? I can't believe it!'

'No, not Lexie.' Emil glanced at his watch, anxiously. 'I gotta go . . . walk Libby. You know how edgy she gets if she doesn't get a jog in over lunch. I'll um, see you later.'

'Oh, okay. Thanks Emil!' I called after him as he dashed off down the hall. I leant back against the door and let a huge smile wash over me. Make a move. How hard could it be?

7

Soundtrack: 'Are You The One?', The Presets
Mood: Wondering just that

Ugly.

Uglier.

Ugliest!

It was 6.50 p.m., and I hated all my clothes, my attempt at hairspray and curlers had transformed me into a cross between low-lying scrub and Krusty the Clown, and the Mega-Lash Mascara had proved considerably more difficult to master than a lifetime of getting-ready movie montages had promised. In fact my montage was less girly excitement and more stress-filled angst. Tonight was the night.

'Finally!' Lexie had moaned, hours earlier when I made the decision. 'You've been superweird around him all week and it's driving me Martin Scorsese!'

'It's turning you into a movie director?' I frowned.

'*Crazy*,' she whispered hoarsely, grasping my shoulders. 'It's driving me CRAZY.'

It was a fair enough call – ever since I'd decided it was Seb, not Justin, who was really the one for me, every moment together had seemed charged. When he examined the Rickenbacker for an invisible scratch, I came over all trembly and dropped the guitar on his new floral-embossed ankle boot. That was after I missed my cue for 'He's Gonna Change' *twice* 'cause I was imagining which moves would look best from his view at the drum kit.

So as I attempted outfit change number four while simultaneously trying to tame my hair into something other than drag queen chic it was pretty much the worst possible time for Dad to emerge from his studio, blinking and covered in specks of red paint, to 'check in' with me.

'Make-up?' He picked up the mascara as though it was an alien test tube. 'I don't know if you're old enough to be wearing this, honey.'

I rolled my eyes. 'Dad, girls at school have nose jobs. Get with it.'

'Excuse me?' Uh-oh. He obviously wasn't in the mood to be told to get with anything – especially 'it'.

'I'm sorry, Daddy,' I whimpered. 'Seb and Lex will be here any minute, and I look like I was raised by wolves.'

'But honey, you agreed to come out with me tonight.'

I stopped fluffing my hair in shock. 'What? Where?'

His eyebrows bunched in confusion. 'To the thing at the art gallery. I asked you weeks ago.'

Weeks ago. Weeks ago I hadn't planned a highly complex series of events that would culminate in Seb and I sharing my first kiss ever and probably being totally in love for the rest of our lives. Weeks ago I had no use for Minty Fresh Breath Spray, but now I had three planted in various locations around the house.

'Oh. Right.' I turned to him nervously. 'I forgot. I'll come to the next one, I promise. I have to see my friends tonight.'

'No, Mia.' His tone was surprisingly firm. 'You spend too much time with your friends as it is. And isn't Lexie the girl who was rude to you when we first moved here?'

I waved my hand dismissively. 'Oh, that's just Lex . . .'

'Well, I don't think that's the sort of friend you should be seeing.'

'You don't even know her, Dad!' My voice rose. 'You don't know anything about us!'

'Mia, I don't want to argue with you . . .'

I was up and shouting. 'And I'm not going to the art gallery with you tonight! I'm almost sixteen, I want to do what almost-sixteen-year-olds do, not what old people do!'

'That's enough, Mia.'

'But you don't understand . . .'

'Enough!'

I threw myself onto my bed, refusing to look at him as he perched awkwardly on the end.

'All right, you don't have to come to the art gallery. But I want you home tonight and studying *alone* – not putting on make-up to see your friends.'

'But Dad . . .'

'No buts. You have plenty of time to see them at school.' He patted my hand, attempting peace. 'Why don't we go downstairs and you can call them while I make some dinner.'

'Sorry, Lex, Dad's pulled the plug . . .' I paced up and down the kitchen as Dad sliced tomatoes, just within earshot. 'It's fair enough, I really need to nail that trig assignment anyway.'

'Your order. Can I take your order . . .'

'Yeah, if you could call Seb that'd be great.'

'This is Pizza Hut. I think you have the wrong number . . .'

'Okay. *Mañana* babe.'

Dad beamed approvingly as I snapped my phone shut. 'I'm proud of you, sweetheart.'

Truth be told, I was pretty proud of me too.

'You look hot, Mia!' Lexie exclaimed as she air-kissed me hello, eyes disco-dancing. 'Doesn't she look hot, Seb?'

'Is that lasagne? I'm starved.' Seb sniffed, wandering in the direction of the kitchen.

'Seb!' barked Lexie. 'I said, doesn't Mia look hot?'

'What?' Seb asked, confused, as I dragged Lexie out on the patio, sliding the heavy glass door shut.

'Ix-nay the obvious omments-cay,' I ordered fiercely.

'You do look hot though,' Lexie nodded approvingly.

'Ya think?' I inspected my reflection critically. 'I'm really nervous.'

'Babe, you're a four-alarm fire,' she drawled. 'He won't be able to resist!'

I grinned at her, my heart racing. 'Time for Phase Two.'

'What are the entertainment options then?' Seb asked, as we squashed together on the couch, pasta bowls balanced in our laps. 'I think there's a Bloc Party special on MTV . . .'

'Actually, I thought we could try this,' I handed him the DVD of *Reality Bites* I'd procured earlier.

'A "wildly romantic comedy"?' Seb inspected the cover. 'Are you cereal?'

'Yeah, it's awesome,' Lexie babbled. 'Winona Ryder plays this chick who ends up with her best friend who's in a band and *ow!*'

She rubbed her ankle as I grabbed the DVD. 'Let's just put it on.'

Right on cue, Lexie's phone 'rang'. 'Mum? I need to come home? Okay.' Like lightning, she was up and grabbing her bag. 'Sorry guys, I gotta jet. Ciao!'

'Bye, Lex!' I called gaily.

'You're going?' Seb looked stunned, a deer caught in crossfire. 'Why? How will I get home?'

'Cab!' yelled Lex as she slammed the door. 'Have fun!'

I smiled at Seb as I snuggled next to him on the couch. 'Guess it's just the two of us.'

He smiled back, thrown. 'Yeah, I guess so.'

'Wow, that was so good!' As a sweet/sad love song played over the rolling credits, I stretched, feeling warm and complete. 'Didn't you love it?'

'Yeah, it was all right,' Seb replied, checking his phone.

'Just "all right"?' I chided. 'I thought it was so romantic and . . . *realistic*. How it ended. With them getting together.'

The credits finished and the screen went black, leaving us lit only by a fat golden moon hanging low over the ocean.

He glanced around. 'Where's the light switch?'

'Let's just sit like this for a while,' I murmured. 'The moonlight's really beautiful, don't you think?'

He turned to look at me, his face only a few inches from mine. His slightly ragged breath brushed my cheek. Our eyes locked and I held my breath. His lips were full and slightly parted as I slowly leant towards him, letting my eyelids close dreamily . . .

'Wait.' He pulled back.

'What's wrong?'

'Mia, I can't.' He got up anxiously.

'Why? What's wrong?'

Seb stumbled over the edge of a rug, backing away from me towards the kitchen. 'I'm sorry, I can't.'

'Why not?' I followed him, bewildered.

He ran his fingers through his hair, unable to look at me. 'I . . . I like . . . someone else.'

'What!' I choked. '*Who?*'

'Mia, I can't . . .' He found his bag and headed for the front door. 'I just can't . . .'

'Seb,' I grabbed his arm, 'just tell me *who.*'

He looked back at me uneasily. 'I *can't.*'

'Tell me!' My voice was shattering into a thousand pieces. 'Seb, *tell me!*'

His eyes rose to meet mine. 'Lexie.'

As the door slammed behind him, the full implication of his confession sank in and I collapsed in tears.

Soundtrack: 'Love for Sale', Faker
Mood: Everything totally sucks

The next day I turned my phone off and chucked a sickie. After spending the morning compiling a list of things wrong with me from my pocket dictionary (*Asexual*: not involved in any sexual activity. *Bizarre*: odd or unusual. *Coward*: a person who is easily frightened and avoids difficult situations), I watched the hour hand creep round to four o'clock, imagining Lexie and Seb waiting for me at rehearsal. Lexie would get out of him what had happened, and he'd be forced to tell her the truth. She'd be A. shocked at first — angry, no doubt — but secretly flattered and B. Vaguely curious. They'd stroll in the late afternoon sun, as possibilities unfolded in their separate imaginations, glances shared and then held. The sun would be sinking into the west as, tentatively, his fingers would reach for hers, and she'd let him and suddenly *everything would feel right*. Their lips would meet cautiously, then passionately, over the sound of crashing waves . . .

I wiped away tears with toilet paper from a fast-diminishing roll. In retrospect, it was obvious. Lexie was the one half the guys in our year wanted — the fact she didn't want them made them want her even more. Lexie was the one who scratched our initials into wet concrete, who snuck us into R-rated movies, for whom rules and laws were *strictly optional*. I tried to be happy for them. I tried to imagine not being upset when they had cute little couple fights and then cute little make-up pash sessions. I tried to tell myself that, really, I was the lucky one – being single meant I'd have all the Fire Fire groupies for myself. But it wasn't working.

'Mia! Mia, wait!'

I ducked and weaved frantically around a stream of lithe dance juniors, hurrying ahead of the voice that gained on me with every step.

'Mia, stop!' Seb grabbed my arm.

I wrenched it back. 'I'll be late for class.'

'Can we talk?' He looked distraught. 'I need to talk to you.'

'Thanks, but I've heard everything you've got to say, Sebastian.' I turned on my heel and marched off.

'This is crazy.' He ran along beside me. 'Mia!'

'Mia? Seb?' In a breathless hurricane of massive sunglasses and tiny shorts, Lexie barrelled around the corner.

'Well, if it isn't the golden couple!' I spat sarcastically.

'Mia, I need to talk to you *in private*,' Seb said urgently, pulling me away from Lexie.

My hands flew to my mouth in mock-drama. 'Oh, haven't you told her I know?' I asked. 'Oh, how awkward! Well, I do!'

'Know what?' Lexie asked.

'Nothing!' insisted Seb.

'That you and Seb are now going out!' I screamed at her.

'THAT IS ENOUGH!' Mrs Kapranos bore down on us and we froze in fear. Her voice dropped to a steely whisper. 'Unless you all want to spend the next month in detention, you will get to class without saying another word.'

We looked at each other, mouths springing open like trapdoors.

'NOT A WORD,' thundered Kapranos. I pushed past the others and bolted.

By hiding out and playing cards in Emil's office (who, BTW, was not at all apologetic that his prediction about Seb was so off the mark), I made it through the day without seeing either of them again. Almost. Guess who was waiting for me by my letterbox like a regular neighbourhood stalker.

'Mia, I know you're mad but I really need to show you something. At my house. It'll explain everything and take *five minutes*.' Seb was onto pleading to get me across the line. '*Please*? For the band?'

His medium-sized white-washed house glowed quietly in the afternoon sun. A brilliant pink bougainvillea stretched lazily up one side, its flowers floating gently in the breeze.

Inside our two pads couldn't have been more different. Somerset Drive was spacious and art-mag modern, yet perpetually full of unwashed dishes and unpaid bills. Seb's house was a home: spotlessly clean, but with life exploding all through it. The walls of the cosy hallway were covered with family photos and kids' toys were stacked tidily in one corner. The smell of rich, garlicky meat lingered in the air. We stood facing each other outside a bedroom door with a Do Not Disturb sign hanging on the doorknob.

'I lied about Lexie — but there is someone else.' He pushed the door open. Standing in his room holding a bottle of hairspray was a tall, striking Greek girl with long dark hair.

'Hi,' she smiled brightly. 'I'm Ella. Seb's sister.'

'You're going out with your sister?' I gagged. 'Seb, that's gross! And I think it's illegal . . .'

'As if!' he exclaimed. 'Ella, get out of my room!'

'Just borrowing this.' She sailed out with the hairspray.

'*This* is who I'm talking about.' He gestured lightly to his bedroom walls. Blu-tacked above the neatly stacked book shelves and alphabetically ordered CD racks were poster after poster of the same come-hither celeb stare. As I turned around slowly, I noticed the largest poster of all, pinned above his bed. *Brokeback Mountain*. Seb's room was a shrine to Jake Gyllenhaal. Reality struck like a bright pink lighting bolt.

'You're gay!'

'It's Jake,' he shrugged. 'Wouldn't you be?'

My world turned inside out. I closed my eyes.

He took a step forward cautiously. 'Are you freaked? Mad?' Then, in deadpan, 'Still completely in love with me?'

I looked up at him in astonishment. For a second I was angry, humiliated, but then he cracked a smile and I knew everything was going to be okay.

'Diet Dr Pepper!' I grasped the bottle Seb handed me from their overflowing fridge. 'I can't believe my gaydar was so off.'

He smiled wryly. 'Everyone's homo-oblivious . . . except for my family, and that's only because . . . well, the details aren't important . . .'

'Mum walked in on him with the boy next door,' Ella swept into the kitchen, a fat baby snuggled on one hip.

'No way!' I spluttered on a mouthful of soft drink.

'It was fairly — ah — dramatic,' Seb hedged.

'She fainted. Had to be taken to hospital. Dad stopped speaking and went home to Greece for an "extended holiday". Greeks, man. What freakin' drama queens. But they're dealing. Nice meeting you, Mia.' She waved the baby's hand at Seb, '*Yia'sou morréh!*'

'*Yia'sou kouklaki!*' he called, as she closed the door behind her. He looked back at me earnestly. 'So, are we okay Mia? I don't want there to be any weirdness.'

'I feel really stupid,' I admitted.

'Hey.' He slung his arm around my shoulders and dropped a kiss on my cheek. 'If I didn't like guys as much as you do, you'd be my perfect girlfriend.'

'Really?' I smiled.

'Sure, why not?' He took my hand. 'C'mon. I'll play you the new drum tracks I'm working on.'

We walked together towards his room. 'So, can me and Lexie make gay jokes now?'

'As long as you never tell *anyone* I nearly kissed a girl. Gross!'

Monday in the a.m. The ever-present Sydney sun had been upstaged by a menacing bank of rolling grey clouds, heavy with the promise of afternoon rain. Kapranos droned on and on about notes from our parents for excursions, and agendas for Social Committee meetings, and what bands had been picked for the Battle of the Bands heat . . .

The whole assembly suddenly woke up.

'I'm glad *something* has your attention,' remarked Mrs Kapranos dryly. 'Before I announce the bands, the organisers want me to pass on how pleased they were with the standard of . . .'

'If we didn't make it, there'll be plenty of other opportunities for us to play,' began Seb diplomatically.

'Are you Martin Scorsese?' Lex whispered ferociously.

Seb frowned. 'Am I that movie director . . .'

'We *have* to get in.' Lexie's eyes were as big as basketballs as she snatched our hands. 'I will *die* if we don't.'

'I'm with you,' I added, squeezing Lexie's hand. We pretended not to look over at the Star Sisters, all shiny waxed legs and clone sunglasses, who were busy pretending not to look over at us. Nikki was wearing the T-shirt Justin had worn at his party. I tried hard not to imagine the circumstances under which she had slipped it over her head.

'And now the moment you've all been waiting for,' Mrs Kapranos read old-person slow from the list. 'Congratulations go to – oh dear – The Boners . . .'

Cue high fives and a chorus of 'dude!' from the pierced and mohawked punk kids up the back.

'. . . Chesterfield . . .'

A hippyish acoustic couple blushed at the polite applause, staring intently at their flower-covered folders.

'Oh yes, I remember these girls from last year's competition: the Star Sisters . . .'

Lexie pretended to be sick as the threesome flicked their hair and preened, giggling at the lame catcalls.

'And . . .'

Lexie gripped my thigh like a vice.

'I can barely read this writing . . .'

Seb made a weird strangling noise. I felt sick, all the air sucked out of me as I squeezed my eyes shut.

'I think that says . . . Fire Fire.'

Lexie screamed. I screamed. Seb punched the air. We were in.

Soundtrack: 'Test Pattern', Damn Arms
Mood: Four coffees and counting

'It totally sucks. Chick newsreaders are always half the age of the dudes. Hit forty and you're yesterday's news.' Lex was on a rant as we burnt up the highway. Rain pounded the windows while the windscreen wipers did double time.

'Totes,' I agreed. '*Quelle* double standard. But your mum is cool . . .'

'Try living with Mommie Dearest.' Lex lit a cigarette. 'That stupid news voice doesn't stop when the cameras do. *This just in, Lexie needs to clean her room.* Puh-lease!'

'Lex, maybe you should slow down.' We whipped past two

cars as she fiddled with the radio. 'Babe, it's pouring — isn't this dangerous?'

'Hey, is that my mobes ringing?'

'Don't answer it now!'

'*Moshi moshi*? Yes, this is her!'

'Lex . . . *Lex!*'

And suddenly she didn't have control of the car. The tyres had locked, and we were sliding across the lane, fast!

'*Mia!*' The phone dropped from her ear and she wrenched the wheel in a panic. But we were racing out of control straight towards a honking truck!

I screamed.

Lexie screamed.

I braced for impact and . . .

I sat bolt upright. I was in the familiar surrounds of my bedroom, dark and alone and petrified. It was a dream. Just a dream. Breathing heavily, I reached for my glass of water and knocked it all over my nightstand. Images flooded my mind: Seb, Lex, Justin, Nikki, Stacey, Sissy, Dad, Emil . . . Out of control, brace for impact . . .

Soundtrack: 'Physical', Macromantics
Mood: Adventurous

'It's so . . . big.'

'I know.'

'I mean, I didn't think they were actually this big.'

'It's totally scary your first time.'

'Gosh, I'm so inexperienced. I wouldn't know where to start.'

'It's dangerous. You can lose track of time, lose your head

completely. But that's why I'm here.' Lexie turned to me emphatically. 'You guys might know music but this, amigos, is *my* speciality. *Malls.*'

When Emil offered to take a band photo of us for the school paper, I was like, 'Yeah, cool', Seb was like, 'Yeah, cool', Lexie promptly dubbed herself band stylist, took our measurements and disappeared off the face of the earth.

'At first I thought it was one of her fads,' I confessed to Seb, as we barred maths homework in lieu of chewing up phone credit. 'You know, like the obsession with tamagotchis...'

'Only speaking in French.' I pictured him twirling an imaginary moustache suavely. '*L'ironie, c'est qu'elle ne parle pas un mot de Français...*'

'Smoking cigars, learning poker,' I thought aloud. 'Oh, and starting that campaign against lime green. For a girl whose idea of commitment is remembering someone's first name, I'm impressed with how much time she's spending making us look good.'

It was pretty much the first time Lexie had dedicated herself to something legal. So when she very seriously asked Seb and I to come shopping with her in order to 'suss our stylistic influences', we had to hide our 'awww' faces in case she reverted to the Lexie of old and smacked us one.

'I can't believe you haven't been to a Westfield before,' she muttered, expertly steering us past fancy menopausal boutiques and kiddy chain stores. 'It's a rite of passage.'

'The biggest store in the Snowy sold farm equipment,' I yawned. 'Tractors got more attention than teenagers.'

'Ha,' smirked Seb. 'Less so-hot-right-now, more hello-stump-jump-plough?'

'Shopping's a drag,' I soapboxed with attitude. 'What's fun about rampant consumerism on a *Saturday*?'

Lex halted us outside a multi-level clothes store pumping rawk music and crawling with coolsies. 'Show me what you like and I'll make a sketch.'

'You bought a sketchpad?' Me and Seb busted out proud parent grins. 'Awww, that's so—OW!'

Lex started by trailing a confident Seb ('gag, hideous, too gay, not gay enough'), leaving me to wander the aisles of distressed denim and high-waisted skirts alone. Okay. Question one: What are your stylistic influences? Hmmm . . . Can I phone a friend? Here I could look like anyone: laid-back beach babe, quirky good girl with an edge, eighties retro queen, or punk-ass princess. Is that why malls were a rite of passage – choose your own identity, with a price tag?

'Can I help ya, sweets?' A big-fringe chick with electric blue eyeliner startled me. Name tag: China.

'I dunno.' I chewed my lip. 'I have to um, pick out some "stylistic influences" . . .'

'Uh-huh.' She snapped gum, rearranging stray T-shirts.

'My friend's making outfits for us . . .'

'Yup.' She looked over my shoulder. Man, I can't even hold the attention of a sales assistant who's *paid* to help me. I slapped my inner forehead. Oh yeah, I'm born to be onstage.

'. . . 'cause, I'm in a band.' I finished weakly.

'You're in a band?' Suddenly she was all ears. 'For real? Whaddya play?'

'Guitar,' I replied nervously.

'Get out!' Her eyes went excited-wide. '*That's freakin' cool*. What are you called?'

'Fire Fire. We're playing in a couple of weeks. At somewhere called the OK Cat Club?'

The girl nodded eagerly. 'That place rocks!' She called out to the other sales girls gossiping idly at the counter. 'Hey guys, c'mere – this chick's in a band! She plays *guitar*!'

Five minutes later everyone working the floor wanted to show me their stuff.

'Do you like this? What about this? These are so cute!' Mini-skirts, boob tubes and hotpants.

'They're a little, ah, revealing,' I hedged.

The girls conferred seriously, experts with hoop earrings.

'Dude, she doesn't want "sexy", she wants "classic but quirky". One Teaspoon, Milk and Honey, Sass and Bide, Lover . . .'

'Right – vintage with a touch of vamp . . .'

'A little eighties, definitely not nineties . . .'

'Interesting necklines, nothing too low-cut, maaaaybe a little lace.'

'Ooh, I see patent kitten heels and printed sockettes! Zing!'

'Stripes, stripes, stripes. Did I say stripes?'

'How do you feel about ditching the all-black thing?' China asked earnestly. 'With your skin tone it's so harsh, and I really think you'd look amazing in blood reds, iridescent blues, even – don't freak out – *metallics*.'

Half-a-dozen sets of made-up eyes turned to me, and I shrugged, smiling. 'I'm in your hands.'

Three different mirrors lit by flattering lighting reflected me saying, 'Wowsers. There're more clothes in here than I actually own.'

'The trick to finding your own look is trying on as many things as humanly possible,' China assured me. 'Enjoy!'

All right, massive pile of clothes I can't afford, I thought to myself. It's just you and me. Let's not make this any harder than it has to be.

But despite my best efforts to hate shopping, it was actually kinda fun wearing something other than basic black. I was feeling it. In fact I was right in the middle of perfecting my best bored-but-beautiful glazed model stare when a volley of familiar giggles rolled in under the change room curtain . . .

'Omigod, did you clock the Nerd Brigade out there?'

'Yeah, they must be hustling for Loser Awareness Day . . .'

'"Give us your change to help us get a date."'

They snickered and I froze, heart hammering. It was Double Trouble.

'Hey does this, like, emphasise neck fat?'

'No, it's cool . . .'

'Really? It doesn't make me look too pudgy around here?'

'Oh, I see . . . maybe a little . . .'

I rolled my eyes. Only walking Barbie dolls could invent neck fat. At least I'd fallen off their radar.

'I wonder where Mousy Mia is . . .'

'I heard this guy mistook her for a surfboard. You know – so *flat* . . .'

'Sissy, as if she'd let another human being on top of her! Hello!?'

And the winner of the Speak Too Soon Award is . . .

'Anyway, speaking of people getting on top of each other, guess who called me in tears this morning . . .'

Who?

'Who?'

'Nikki.'

Nikki!

'For real?'

'It seems all is not well in the land of Miss Moretti and our dear brother . . .'

My eyes popped, jaw dropped. Really!? Did he . . .

'. . . dump her? Sissy, stop holding out on me! What'd she say . . .'

A dramatic pause on the other side of the curtain. I held my breath. *Puh-lease* say they're over . . .

'Hey, Miz, you finito or what?' Lexie blew into the change room with gale force. 'Lemme see that milkshake, bizatch!'

Rule Number One When Attempting to Eavesdrop: Leave loudmouthed friends behind!

'All is not well. That's what she said?'

'For the gazillionth time, Lex, YES!'

After making the hastiest change room exit in history, we were elbow-deep in Justin Timberlake-style fedora hats in the men's section of Myer — a stylistic influence Seb had insisted upon — sipping takeaway coffees and playing detective.

'So,' I asked with bated breath, 'has the jury reached a decision?'

'He dumped her,' Lex burped. 'Deffo.'

'I concur,' nodded Seb. 'Love is like . . . a latte. Gets your heart pumping at first, but what starts hot soon turns cold.'

'Confucius say: stick to Diet Dr Pepper?' I asked, and Seb nodded wisely as his phone blasted out Beyoncé.

'Ladies, I must love you and leave you,' he announced. 'Apparently shopping is no excuse when it comes to cleaning up the breeders' mess.'

'Huh?'

'Babysitting my baby brother Theo.' He straightened his tie. 'Luckily, you're never too young to learn the ancient art of accessorising. Today I begin the hats and gloves chapter — raw silk is in, lambs wool is out, nothing in blue, everything vintage.' We nodded in serious approval. 'Now, listen here, Miss Mannix,' he continued, chucking me under the chin. 'You've gotta get your mojo on with the now-available-at-a-party-near-you Justin! You are the dictionary definition of cool, and the sooner you embrace it, the better.'

'Now's the time to pounce, pussycat,' Lexie purred saucily, pulling a vixen pose. 'Meow!'

Seb bailed, clocking a vacantly cute sales guy on his way out and giving us a thumbs up. We giggled, and then we were two.

'True or false,' Lex announced. 'We could both totally smash a hot fudge sundae, with extra fudge and extra sundae, right now.'

There's nothing like a calorie-fest after a hard day's shop. 'True!'

We linked arms. 'The only question is: Coffee Toffee Crunch or White Chocolate Cheesecake . . . ?'

'Excuse me girls.' Heavy hands clamped down on our shoulders. 'Can I check your bags please?' A large security guard resembling a cross between a dump truck and a pit bull was regarding us suspiciously. My stomach sank when I saw that absolutely all the colour had drained out of Lexie's face.

The guard poked disinterestedly through my stuff, his eye trained on a nervous Lex. Her hands were sweaty as she clutched my arm.

'And yours?'

Reluctantly, she opened her huge shoulder bag.

'I s'pose you were going to pay for these.' The gruff guard produced an expensive-looking pair of round silver cufflinks, set with a clear amber stone, from the disarray of Lexie's belongings.

'They're for . . . her boyfriend.' She blurted, pointing at me. 'He's, uh, gonna be back any second to pay for them.'

The guard's face took 'disbelieving' to a whole new level.

I nodded slowly, as if in a dream. 'He'll be . . . right . . . back.'

'Well, your "boyfriend" has exactly ten seconds to appear or I'm calling the police.'

I stared at Lexie. Petty crime? The cops? When had our afternoon turned into an episode of *Law & Order*? I flashed on me and Lex making a run for it and becoming wayward teen versions of Thelma and Louise: young and crazy and living life on the run. I could change my name, wear a wig, speak in a husky voice. *I'm Blondie, wanted in five different states, what's it to ya?*

'Well,' the guard pressured. 'Is this boyfriend gonna make an appearance or . . .'

'Babe.' A strong hand slipped into mine and smoky-smelling stubble brushed my cheeks in a kiss. 'You got those cufflinks?'

It was Justin.

Under the disbelieving glare of the security guard, Justin nonchalantly handed over his plastic to pay for the $300 cufflinks. His hand was still in mine, thumb rubbing the inside of my palm slowly, causing waves of shuddery desire to threaten my equilibrium.

'Dollface, I'm stoked you remembered my dad's birthday.' He brushed the hair out of my eyes. 'It's so sweet of you.'

I smiled timidly into his dark, chocolate-brown eyes, allowing my gaze to drop for a second to the mischievous smile pulling at his lips. Seb's words floated back to me. *Mojo.* It was time.

As he pocketed his plastic, I leant in to finger his jacket collar, tipping my face up to his. 'So,' I murmured. 'I can think of something way more fun than shopping that we can do this afternoon.'

It was his turn to look surprised. 'Oh yeah?'

I closed my eyes and leant in towards him, till my mouth was only inches from his. 'But I have band practice,' I whispered, 'so it'll have to wait.'

And just like that, I turned and sauntered off.

'And then Mia's like, "Loverboy, let's blow off shopping so I can blow you."'

'I did not!' I kicked a roll of gaffer tape at her. 'Less porno, more *playful*.'

'And then they did it, right there on the floor.' Lex straddled the mic stand. 'Oh Justin, baby, I want you so bad, oh yeah, touch me there . . .'

'Sexually frustrated much, Lex?' Seb spoke through a toothpick as he assembled cymbals with the precision of a surgeon.

As she humped enthusiastically, a silver hipflask bounced to the ground and we all exchanged *those* kind of glances.

'Well, you're looking very Youth Gone Wild today,' Seb muttered.

'Thank you.'

'That wasn't a compliment.'

She sneered at him, bringing the flask to her lips and taking a deliberate swig.

I could see Seb biting his tongue as he redirected the conversation with the spin of a cymbal. 'Sounds like you had some serious mojo working, girlfriend.'

I flushed. 'It was no big.' Actually, it really, really, really was, and it was bordering on obsessive exactly how many times I'd replayed That Scene in my mind. Even throughout my 'meeting' with Rocho about my less-than-stellar life drawing assignment, the Smoky Stubbly One had been the source of a million accidental daydreams. Grades schmades: I could rock guitar, help write semi-decent songs, and successfully pull off a PG-rated seductive act. Why wasn't there a merit system for that?

'So, has he really broken up with Nasty Nik?' Seb tossed me a cable.

'Rumble in the playground jungle says affirmative,' I nodded, unravelling cord around a still-humping Lexie. 'He is single and ready to mingle.'

'What a co-inky dink!' Seb exclaimed in mock-surprise. 'So are you!'

I pulled out my Mafioso voice. 'The lesson here is, crime *does* pay.'

Seb took it like a Mafia kingpin. 'Oh yeah, I fuggut to ask the wise guy over here.' He raised an eyebrow at Lexie. 'Cufflinks? Who are you, freakin' James Bond?'

She tapped out a cigarette and shrugged petulantly, the no-way-naïve blonde. 'I'm an impulsive shopper.'

Seb frowned. 'Lex, you can't smoke in here. It's a *rehearsal studio*.'

She tossed him a faux-innocent smile. 'Guess I'll have to go outside then. Call me when you're ready to start!'

As the door slammed, Seb narrowed his eyes. 'No wonder everyone wants to be the singer.' His sticks skittered across the skins in annoyance. 'What was it last week: "The face of the band can't break a sweat". And you know she hasn't got all her parts down.'

'She will,' I replied, only half believing it. 'Besides, I bet our outfits are amazing.'

'What would be "amazing" is if *she* set up her keyboard instead of *you*.'

'It only takes a minute.'

Just then, Lexie's phone started ringing. Loudly. Seb looked ready to snap so I snatched at Lexie's bag to shut it off. I'm still getting the hand-eye coordination thing down — the contents of her bag shook out everywhere.

'Damn!' I bent down to scrape up her crap: unpaid parking fines, chewed-up leaky pens, used lip-gloss tubes and . . .

'Is that Lex?' I stared in disbelief at the tattered photo.

Seb glanced over my shoulder and snorted. 'Remember how I said she used to make Snow White look like a delinquent? That's Nicole — Nikki — next to her.'

He wasn't kidding.

The two young girls in the photo stood behind a large pale-pink cake proudly holding a Second Prize ribbon. Lexie's hair was brushed and cut into a sweet bob, her Peter Pan-collared blouse was tucked into a skirt that fell modestly below the knee. There was no hard glint in her eye, no secret plan hidden behind her smile. In short, she looked nothing like my shoot-'em-up Lex at all. A picture of posture beside her, Nicole's smile was shot with silver braces, boobs hidden behind a bulky jumper. They were a pastel pastiche: pre friendship-wars, broken hearts, and girl-world bitchiness. I was staring through time at two girls who probably liked cutting out pictures of horses and idolised their mothers. What happened to these friends? Did growing up simply mean growing apart? Or was there a secret, vicious fall-out, coloured by bitter betrayal and bad blood, about to happen in the days and months that followed? As I stared at the naïve pair in the picture, the thought suddenly struck me: *was I next?*

A 21:00 rendezvous at my house was planned before the photo shoot. Given Dad's week-long absenteeism (he was basically living in his studio trying to crack a concept for a new series of portarits) we should have been in the clear. But when the sound of crashing Russian classical music greeted me halfway up the drive, I realised I'd have to change tack. Sal Mannix was in breakthrough mode. Which pretty much meant run for cover.

'Jeez, Louise.' I couldn't help but laugh, as I followed the sound of booming music into the kitchen. The man was cooking.

'Mia!' he shouted happily over the music, up to his elbows in flour. 'You're home!'

'And you're making ravioli.' I approached the chaos cautiously. 'I guess that means—'

'Breakthrough, darling, breakthrough!' He enveloped me in a floury hug, words tumbling forth in childlike enthusiasm, 'I was thinking too small! Large-scale photographs. Floor to ceiling. *Hand painted.* Day colours, sun colours! Pore over every pore. *Break down* the portrait concept by blowing it out of proportion – literally!' And he was off and racing, art babble that made no sense to anyone but him. The only thing to do was simply wait it out.

'And so,' he raced back to the kitchen as a buzzer sounded, flinging open a smoke-filled oven. 'I thought we'd have some people over for dinner. Invite your friends!'

'Tonight?'

'Why not?' He threw back a mouthful of red wine, doing a madcap little dance. 'No time like the present! Seize the day! *Carpe diem* . . .'

'Actually, Dad, I have a ridiculous amount of homework to get through . . .'

'Oh pish-posh!' he exclaimed, chopping onions with a crazed, haphazard vigour. 'Let's have dinner — I don't know how your classes are going, what assignments you're acing! I only ever know you're home when you play that, um, "music", that, you know . . .' His hands fluttered as his words stumbled.

In his talk-first-think-later babble, I could see he hadn't meant to insult me, but there was no disguising his disrespect for my chosen bedroom soundtracks. I cocked my head at him pointedly.

He feigned naivety, ending with, 'We haven't caught up in weeks!'

'Well, Dad, considering my life revolves around a band you don't deem as real art — an attitude I find upsetting and aggravating — that's not surprising,' is what a braver girl might have said. Instead, I offered a watery smile and a, 'Next time, Dad. Have fun.' After all, I had bigger fish to fry.

10

Soundtrack: 'Sell Yourself', Lost Valentinos
Mood: Riding wolves barefoot

We were hyped up on nerves and naughtiness as Emil zoomed through sleeping suburban streets, climbing up and out of the neon-bright city. A tight-lipped Lex wouldn't show us the clothes, and Emil wouldn't tell us the clandestine location of the photo shoot, so there was nothing else to do but watch the world fly by. As Libby scrabbled happily in my lap, I felt full of thrill and art and life itself. Taking a band photo — committing our image to paper — made everything real. *We were really doing it!*

I wound down the window and yelled at the darkened houses, lit only by the flickering reflection of TV screens inside, little electric-blue fires. We shot through green lights like a stray bullet and everywhere was adventure.

'This is it.' Before Emil had even pulled to a complete stop Fire Fire were tumbling out and racing to the view.

'Wow.'

The whole world spread out before us: a huge glittering carpet of twinkling lights, as far as the eye could see. A join-the-dots puzzle with a million different answers. I stretched my hands out wide and shut my eyes, cool night air rushing my face, feeling free, free, free. Lexie twirled cartwheels and Libby ran between her twisting hands and feet, yapping excitedly.

'It's . . . amazing,' I breathed happily to Emil. 'How did you find this place?'

'I bury the bodies of my enemies up here.'

'Ooh, you're bad,' I teased.

'Better believe it.'

Lexie, Seb and Libby disappeared down the path, but we remained side by side, above it all, the spread of houses below ignorant of our watch over them.

I tried to put my thoughts into words. 'Every light is a place full of people, each with just as many hopes and fears and dreams as everybody else. Everyone sees things differently, but there they are, all together . . . Sort of puts things into perspective, hey?'

'Yeah,' he agreed. 'There're so many secrets out there.'

A chorus of chirruping crickets were the only sounds around us. I felt part of the night, connected to all the magic and mystery hidden in the stars.

'Emil, thanks for doing this for us.' My words suddenly blurted in freefall. 'Not just this, everything. You've been such a great friend ever since I got here, and it really . . . It means a lot to me.'

I hugged him hard, and he hugged me back in surprise, awkwardly at first, but as I tightened my arms around his neck our bodies softened into each other, fitting comfortably like jigsaw pieces, my head resting easily against his chest. He smelled like boy deodorant: musky and clean. His thin body was as long as the land and warm through a cotton T-shirt. I pulled back, but somehow our faces stayed close together. His head dipped down to mine, our foreheads almost touching. My breath quickened as his hand rose to touch my face and instinctively I pushed my cheek against it, his touch light and gentle. I opened my eyes to see him looking at me seriously, green eyes framed by long lashes, and I remembered the last time someone gazed back at me like that — *Justin* — and I was back on earth with a jolt and pulling away from him in confusion.

'I'm sorry, Mia, that was stupid of me . . .'

'No, no, don't be sorry.'

'This wasn't the right time . . .'

I touched my cheek where his fingers had just been, my mind racing. 'No, it's not that . . .'

He swallowed hard, tense. 'Have you thought about it?'

'About what?'

Lexie's voice floated from the distance. 'Mia, c'mere!'

'About you and me . . .'

I blinked. 'Not really.'

Lexie yelled again, '*Mia!*'

'Yeah. That's fine.' He turned to walk to the car.

'Wait, Emil, that's not to say . . .'

Lexie jogged up and waved me over impatiently. 'Showtime!'

She paced behind a picnic table laden with three garbage bags, lit harshly by light from a nearby toilet block. 'Okay, so, I really don't know if you guys will like these . . .'

'I'm sure they're awesome,' I said. Be cool, Mannix. Now's so not the time to spill.

'You don't have to wear any of this if you don't want to . . .'

Seb shrugged off his jacket. 'We won't.'

'If you hate them, that's completely understandable.' Lexie bit her nail anxiously.

'Lexie, are you all right?' Seb stared at the jumpy Lex in fascination. 'Could it be . . . Surely not . . .'

'What?' She crossed her arms huffily.

Seb grinned in delight. 'Don't tell me you're *nervous*!'

'Gasp!' I deadpanned. 'She actually cares what we think. I'm gonna have to sit down.'

'Shut up! Just . . . just . . . oh, whatever.' She grabbed her bag and stalked off. Me and Seb exchanged stunned game-show-contestant faces and followed her into the toilets. I glanced over my shoulder at Emil setting up lights. He didn't look back.

'C'mon Mia, show me!' Lexie banged on the toilet door impatiently.

'Seb, are you dressed?' I asked.

'Uh . . . yeah . . .'

'Let's come out together then.'

'Okay. One . . . two . . .'

'Three!' I unlocked the door and faced my bandmates. Lexie smiled hopefully. Seb burst out laughing. I wanted to curl up and die. It was a neon and gold punk party, but only one of us was on the guest list. Seb's standard issue tight black jeans and retro sunnies looked cool, but the outlandish bright-pink T-shirt emblazoned with a massive I AM SEX couldn't have been less Seb than my teeny-tiny metallic gold playsuit complete with ripped pink stockings, two armfuls of metal bracelets and patent black heels.

Lexie, of course, looked ridiculously hot in a stiffly layered pink tutu, black lace bra under a see-through white singlet, topped off with a gold tiara shoved into teased blonde hair.

'Are you going to wear the wig, Mia?' Her overly polite tone was way at odds with her crazy get-up.

'There's a wig?' spluttered Seb. 'Put it on! For Jake's sake, put it on!'

'I think black hair matches better than pink,' I stuttered, shooting him a *shut-the-hell-up* glare. The hairpiece in question looked like a diseased flamingo had chosen my head as its final resting ground.

'You don't like it?' Lexie's face fell. 'You hate it. You both hate it all.'

'No, no, we love it!' Alarmed at the sight of a potential melt-down, I squeezed her arm encouragingly. 'It must have cost you a fortune. Where did you find everything?'

'I made them.'

'You're kidding, you made all this?' Seb exclaimed. 'Even the jeans?'

I looked at our outfits with renewed respect. 'Lex, that's incredible. I had no idea you could sew like this.'

'I can fix the sizes if they're wrong.' She perked up. 'I can take things in.'

I shifted uneasily. 'Let's just take the photo and then maybe we can change them . . .'

'What?'

Seb interrupted quickly. 'Make some *minor adjustments* later. C'mon kids. Time to look moody and apathetic!'

'Cool,' Lexie beamed happily, as we headed out. 'How fun is this!?'

Oh yeah. This was gonna be way fun.

11

Soundtrack: 'Shadowland', Youth Group
Mood: What? Oh, um . . . Distracted

'Mia. *Mia Mannix.*'

'Huh?' I landed back to Planet Art Class. 'Wh-what?'

Rocho sighed impatiently as the rest of the class snick-ered. 'If you'd been paying attention, you'd know we've been discussing which artist your end-of-term work will be an interpretation of.'

The days leading up to our gig at the OK Cat Club had been speeding by as if Lexie was behind the wheel. I was on no sleep – somehow the universe conspired for the Battle of the Bands heat to be at the end of the busiest week at school ever, including today's deadline that naturally, I'd completely forgotten about.

As I rose shakily to my feet, my mind made tracks like a deranged moth racing round a light, desperately grasping for an answer that didn't exist. My gaze flitted to Emil. He looked away.

'Yves Klein,' I blurted out, remembering the picture above Emil's desk. 'The French guy.'

'And what interests you about his work?'

'I like his take on making art,' I hedged. 'Using women as human paintbrushes. Making the process of creating art part of the art itself . . . It's really interesting.'

'And so what will your work be?'

'My work? What will my work be?'

Rocho regarded me with suspicion. 'That's what I just asked, Mia.'

'It'll be . . . I'm going to . . .' My eyes skated around the classroom, trying to find something — anything — to hang an answer on. They landed on a Guerrilla Girls poster — feminist art activists who pointed out that less than five per cent of the artists in the Modern Art section of the Metropolitan Museum in New York were women, but eighty-five per cent of the nudes were female. Cue lightbulb-above-head moment:

'I'm going to reverse the gender polarity,' I stated confidently. 'Women's bodies are on display enough as it is! I say it's time the guys got covered in paint!'

'All right!' The girls in the class cheered. The guys shifted, unsure of whether to embrace this unconventional chance to get nude or not.

'Sweet,' shrugged Michael with a lazy grin, and instantly the lads were in.

'Well, we all look forward to that, Mia.' Rocho's eyebrows were still raised as I sunk down in relief, glancing at Emil with a grin. Usually he'd be shaking his head at me, mouthing something about being a fraud. But instead he stared straight ahead, pointedly ignoring me. My eyes narrowed — admittedly the photo shoot had been awkward, but there was no way I was gonna let things end like that. Ripping a sheet of paper from my art diary I quickly scribbled a message: *Demonstrate yr commitment to Fire Fire this Thursday! Meet me front of the OK Cat Club at 7.* The scrunched-up note bounced lightly onto his desk. He uncurled it like a treasure map. A minute late I had my reply. *OK, Kitty. I'm committed.*

The afternoon before the heat, we cut class for OBF: Operation Band Fash. In Lexie's mind that meant 'minor adjustments', in Seb's and mine, 'complete overhaul'. But we knew we had to handle things delicately . . .

'Just say it to my face — *you hate them*!' Lexie sobbed loudly from inside Seb's ensuite.

'Lexie, that's not what we're . . .'

'Yes it is!' She wrenched open the door. Running mascara had transformed her into a heavy-metal-loving clown. 'You wanna totally change them!'

'We want to *evolve* them . . .'

'You hate them! I HATE YOU.' She slammed the door and locked it. Something smashed.

Seb scratched his head. 'Tim Tam?'

I leafed through the baby magazines on the kitchen counter as Seb arranged some Double Coat Tim Tams on a plate next to two glasses of low-fat milk.

I jerked my head in the direction of the bathroom. 'Any ideas, O Wise One? I'm out.'

Seb squeezed his eyes shut and massaged his temples. I took the opportunity to inhale a Tim Tam. Suddenly his eyes flew open and a smile raced across his face. 'I believe the word is *snap*.'

'I know, I feel stupid too,' I admitted, sinking onto Seb's bed. 'I'm just not brave enough for those outfits.'

'Those *incredible* outfits,' Seb added, in a booming voice. 'They're light years ahead of us.'

'I'm just way too chicken to get up onstage in them!' I exclaimed. 'It's totally my fault we want to change them.'

'Bolder people wouldn't.' Seb shook his head sadly.

'C'mon, Seb. Let's tell the organisers Fire Fire can't play . . .'

We shuffled towards the door as Seb mouthed at me, 'Five, four, three, two . . .'

Right on cue, Lex slowly unlocked the bathroom door. 'Is that true? That *you're* the thing that's wrong with the clothes?'

Swallowing our pride, we nodded in unison. 'Yup.'

She narrowed her eyes. 'Really? Don't lie, you guys.'

Seb and I steeled ourselves.

'Lex, do you remember the first time you went shopping on your own?' I began cautiously. 'What did you buy?'

'A gay frilly dress I wore once then chucked out,' she answered, equally cautiously. 'No offence on the gay bit, Seb.'

'And do you remember the first few songs Mia wrote?' Seb took over. 'How whiny and I-want-a-guy-I-can't-have they were?'

'Hey . . .' I interjected.

'Yeah, they did suck,' Lexie mused. 'They were *really* gay.'

'Guys, I'm right here,' I exclaimed.

'But then she rewrote them a couple of times and *voila*,' Seb held his hands up, 'some pretty decent I-want-a-guy-I-can't-have songs.'

'What about the first crush Seb had,' I shot back. 'The guy in the Big W catalogues? Lame!'

Seb pointed at me accusingly. 'Hey, you don't know perfection when you see it . . .'

'Okay, okay,' Lexie interrupted. 'If you've got a point, hurry up and make it.'

Seb sounded serious. 'Lex, you're a really good designer. This could even be – dare I say it – *your thing,* in the same way that falling for intellectually challenged rock guys is Mia's thing and being ridiculously good-looking is my thing.'

'But,' I continued, choosing to ignore the snipe at Justin, 'the thing with having a *thing* is, it's hard work . . .'

'And it doesn't always go your way.' Seb looked at us both honestly. 'Fire Fire isn't always gonna win competitions and be everyone's favourite band. People will hate us, and be jealous of how attractive I am.'

Enough was enough. 'Look Lex — crying in the bathroom because we need to make some changes to your designs is really childish,' I announced. 'Working *with* us is what a real designer would do.'

The die had been cast. The sword thrown down. She regarded us both gravely. We looked back, equally serious.

Suddenly she threw her head back, snarling like a jungle cat, 'Nice speech, but you can still go to hell!' She slammed the bathroom door, hard.

We looked at each other stunned, sick. That was *not* how that was supposed to . . .

Lexie opened the door, grinning. 'You guys, I'm kidding!!'

And so Lexie was an angel for the rest of OBF (if angels suck down cigs and swear like troopers). We traded ripped pink stockings for modest black leggings, high heels for comfy Cons and an armful of bracelets for just one. No further talk of the dead flamingo, but, like a true artist, on some things there was simply no compromise.

'The playsuit is indie music's answer to Madonna's pointy cone bra,' she insisted. 'It's *iconic*.'

'You do have great stems, babe,' drawled Seb.

'Plus, Justin's brain will explode when he sees it!'

As much as it freaked me out, I decided the playsuit could have its day in the sun.

Seb informed us that over time his pink shirt would burn holes in our retinas and strip us of the power of sight, so Lexie graciously agreed to whip him up a skinny pink tie to wear with a white collared shirt instead.

After OBF was signed off at 17:00 hours, OBM (Operation Band Makeover) began. My knowledge of girl tools started with mascara and ended with lip-gloss, but apparently there was far, far more to it than that. Lexie dumped all sorts of shimmers, glimmers and eyebrow rimmers on Seb's bed and set to work.

As she inspected five different foundations on her hand with the critical eye of a nuclear physicist, my mind drifted to tonight. Sound check was at seven – I'd never done a proper sound check before . . .

'What's going on with Emil?'

I flinched, feeling liquid eyeliner streak towards my temple.

'Huh? What do you mean?'

Seb glanced at Lex in something like anticipation as she wet a Kleenex. 'Things seemed weird at the shoot,' she said 'casually'.

I sighed. 'We had a . . . moment.'

'A pash moment?' They leant towards me, puppies straining at their leashes.

I frowned. 'No, more a hug that turned into a stare that turned into a me freakin' out moment.'

'Ha!' Lexie grinned at Seb. 'No tonsil hockey. Cough it up!'

'Damn you, Mannix,' Seb plucked a crisp ten-dollar note from his wallet. 'Surrender the rock star fantasy already! What's wrong with nerd boy?'

'Nothing's wrong with him . . . But nothing's right with him either.' I shook my head, trying to clear my thoughts.

Sure, I'd thought about it — but I was super-cautious of manufacturing another non-existent crush after almost ruining my entire friendship with Seb. I knew I could probably talk myself into liking Emil, but that didn't make it real. We worked as friends — I just couldn't see us working as a couple. And at the end of the day, Justin Jackson was the one my imagination started playing with when my head hit the pillow every night. *That* was real.

I flicked a hair elastic at Seb. 'Has someone not been paying attention? Me and Justin are on the verge of being together in a forever kind of way.'

'Look, granted, Emil wouldn't look out of place at a *Star Trek* convention, and his dress sense is . . . an unusual take on vintage chic,' Seb offered diplomatically. 'But the whole brooding rock boy thing reaching *boyfriend* status? Forget it.'

'Why?' I asked, bewildered. Seb had been with more guys than me — his advice was gospel.

'Honey, you're a garden variety romantic.' Seb replied matter-of-factly, 'You're all about flowers and "your song" and a guy who'll stick around after you've done the deed. Justin Jackson is the boy equivalent of a Sofia Coppola film: complicated, moody, looks great, but when all is said and done, no cheesy happy ending.'

Wowsers. Was I really holding out for a completely unrealistic Hollywood ending, starring Justin Jackson as Fantasy Lover? Was my life actually one of those complicated art-house films shot in black and white where it's not about love at all, it's about being detached and hip and drinking espressos with weird Europeans boys with amusingly obscure interests. Admittedly this was a film far better suited to a culture snob like Emil . . .

'Just think about it is all.' Seb's voice cut into my reverie. 'I don't wanna see you get hurt. Now, while you ladies uphold capitalism's stranglehold over womankind, I'm going on a dinner run. Requests?'

As soon as he was out of earshot Lexie threw her blush brush down. 'Don't listen to him. Jackson's not a fantasy, he's totally landable.'

'Really?' Lexie was an expert! Her word was also gospel! 'How?'

She sat down opposite me excitedly. 'Okay. Lesson uno. How would you answer if Justin asked if you had a boyfriend?'

'I'd tell him the truth: no,' I replied with conviction. 'No way, no how . . .'

Lexie shook her head emphatically. 'That, my friend, is an *instant fail*!' She cleared her throat with an air of authority. 'Why are designer threads more desirable than Kmart cut-price?'

I sighed. 'Pop philosophy based on chain stores is not the answer here, Lex . . .'

'Because they're *harder to get*,' she continued. 'Boys like *the chase* — it all goes back to when they used to hunt, like, kangaroos and stuff.'

'Justin's not actually indigenous . . .'

'You have to be *unavailable*,' Lexie exclaimed. '*Designer*, not 7-Eleven.'

'7-Eleven?' I asked meekly.

'Open 24 hours for your convenience,' she smirked. 'If he asks you about another guy, *this* is what you should do . . .'

The smell of pizza drifting down the hallway heralded Seb's return.

'What up, y'all? I got vego, I go— SWEET GYLLENHAAL!'

His look was stunned mullet. 'Mia, what in Jake's name happened to your hair?'

'Is it that bad?'

Lexie finished snipping, nonplussed. 'Chillax, dudes, asymmetrical haircuts are *a la carte.*'

'I believe you mean *a la mode.*' Seb inspected my black tufts critically. 'It looks like you tried to cut chewing gum out in the dark.'

Lexie snapped her fingers at him. 'Perfect excuse for your dad, Miz.' She dragged me into the bathroom. 'Get ready to meet the new Mia Mannix.'

'Well,' Lexie asked breathlessly, 'What do you think?'

I stared at my reflection. Were my eyes really that big? My skin that . . . glowing? Since when did I have cheekbones? And my hair . . . And the outfit . . .

'Hurry up and say something,' she squealed.

'C'mon, Mannix, the suspense is killing Lexie's appetite,' Seb added dryly.

The girl in the mirror began to smile: I was officially a certified coolsie.

'I love it!' I turned to the others confidently. 'Let's go make rock'n'roll history.'

Lexie whooped through a large mouthful of pizza as Seb straightened his tie momentously. 'Or at the very least a well-written footnote. Either way, I'm in.'

Sound check was an exercise in setting levels and humiliation. We were trying to be all, 'Yeah, we've done this, like, a billion times', until someone had to show us how to turn the mics on.

'Last time the switch was in a different place,' I explained to the soundie sporting a greasy ponytail and 'Rock is Dead' T-shirt.

He flicked the switch, unimpressed. 'Maybe you should let your boyfriend set it up.'

'I don't *have* a boyfriend,' I retorted, realising as soon as it was out of my mouth that I sounded less sisters-doing-it-for-themselves and more all-by-myself-a-la-Bridget-Jones. Nice one Mannix.

Before we knew it, the eerily empty room we'd been mucking around in opened its doors and began filling up with kids from Silver Street and beyond. Pale punks held together by Sex Pistols patches and safety pins rubbed shoulders with gentle twee-pop couples, blinking behind matching coke bottle glasses. Star Sister wannabes rolled their fake-eyelash-heavy eyes at the distracted art nerds inspired by pretty much everything, while pretty dancers who didn't drink chatted with sleazy actors who did, and a whole collection of randoms ambled in to slouch in posses and scope out each other. Cries of 'Dude, you look hot/cool/wasted' bounced off walls sticky with stale sweat.

We'd drawn the short straw of going last, so, with time and nerves to kill, we pushed our way through the crowds to the refuge of backstage, flashing armbands at the fat security set who'd seen it all before.

As soon as we walked into the tiny band room, we instantly wished we hadn't.

'Well, well, well. If it isn't the Mousketeers.'

Three sets of shimmery cat eyes narrowed at us from under identical snow-white wigs. Their body-hugging silver leotards wouldn't have looked out of place on an ice rink.

Stop the presses, hell *had* frozen over and it'd already got a floorshow.

'The Mousketeers spawned Britney Spears,' Seb answered calmly. 'Isn't that who you're ripping off?'

Sissy glanced at our outfits disparagingly. 'It's a shame the person who dressed you wasn't blessed with the gift of sight.'

Lexie lunged, and everyone jumped as we grabbed her.

'Keep your dog on a leash or I'll get it put down,' Nikki spat.

'Five minutes, girls.' Greasy Ponytail ogled the flesh on display.

'What's your problem, Moretti?' Lexie exclaimed as the three swished past us.

'Forget it, Lex,' we muttered, easing the quivering blonde away from the door.

'No, seriously.' She stood her ground. 'A long time ago we used to be friends. What did I do to make you hate me so much?'

Nikki spun back, eyes glittering with something hidden. 'You didn't do anything, Lexie. You didn't do anything at all.'

Curiosity killed the kitty and got the better of Fire Fire, so we snuck back out to watch the Star Sisters show. Well hidden in a shadowed back corner, we stood shoulder-to-shoulder, arms folded, ready to despise.

The lights dimmed dramatically and a naff pop beat kicked in. The three witches pranced onstage to a chorus of hoots and whistles. With frozen 'sexy' smiles plastered on their faces they began what could best be described as a combination of a gym routine, a strip show and an epileptic fit. Their first song was actually called 'The Special is Boy Soup'.

'Oh, please,' I groaned. 'They're not even playing any instruments!'

'As long as they perform to original music, it doesn't matter.' Seb pointed out. 'Even though that track didn't even graduate from primary school.'

'Any more of this and I'm gonna be sick,' Lexie gagged. 'This is a *rock show*. I'm gonna find the fun.'

My sidekicks split as the Star Sisters' first song ended in a flashy formation dancing pose, hands outstretched, breasts heaving, sweat lightly spotting their still-smiling faces. Is this actually what guys want — walking racks, personality optional? Girls who think climate change is about next season's bikini? Surely not my kinda guys. Surely not . . .

'Justin.' There he was, not ten metres in front of me, smoking next to a No Smoking sign, eyes trained on one girl. Well, at least he's not into incest. For the rest of the set, I watched him watching Nasty Nikki's every twist and every turn.

A seething mob of The Boners look-alikes replaced the Star Sister's fans at the front of the stage as ear-splitting, three-chord, punk rock ripped through the crowd. I was standing in the shadows, fighting nerves and trying to pick one song from the next, when I felt someone watching me. Looking round, my eyes locked with Emil's. A bud in the building! I moseyed on over.

'What's what, amigo?'

He looked at me like I was a boring stranger at a party desperate to make chit-chat.

'Hey,' I tried again. 'How's it going?'

He pointed to his ears and shrugged, mouthing, 'Can't hear you.'

Screw this. This was my first gig ever and I was so not wasting it on friendship dramas.

We faced off in a corridor backstage, muffled music from the stage thumping loudly.

'What's the deal?' I demanded.

He pulled a scrunched-up piece of paper from his pocket and handed it to me. 'I waited for you . . .'

The note. The meet-me-at-seven note. Damn! Damn damn damn! 'Ohmigod, I totally forgot. I'm so sorry . . .'

'It's cool . . .'

'No, it's not, there were just so many things to do, and Lexie almost freaked out, and I didn't know how to turn the amp on . . .'

'It's all right'

'And the sound guy was really mean to me, and the Star Sisters were really mean to us, and . . .'

'Mia . . .'

'And we're gonna suck! Who am I kidding, I can't play guitar! People are gonna laugh at us and . . .'

'Mia! Stop!' He clamped his hand over my still-rambling mouth. 'You have to calm down, okay? Are you calm?'

Eyes wide, I nodded as he slid his hand away slowly. From onstage I could hear wild applause as The Boners finished their set.

'I'm sorry I stood you up,' I whispered. 'The only word is "mortified". I would die if someone did that to me.'

He smiled. 'Lucky for you, you've kind of got the best excuse in the world right now.'

'Oh man, it's been crazy.' I was getting wired, I could feel it. 'I'm so nervous I feel like throwing up.'

'Well, you and your haircut look amazing.' His eyes showed he meant it.

I felt a sudden thrill from his interest, and without thinking moved into flirt mode. 'You think so? It's not, like, too much?'

'It's magazine-cover worthy, trust me.' He shoved his hand deep into his pocket. 'I have something for you.' Luckily it was G-rated — one of those clear plastic eggs you get in the little vending machines outside supermarkets. Inside was a pink plastic ring with *Good Luck!* in a cute scrawly font stamped onto it.

From onstage came the sweet strains of a hippy-trippy couple finding love via acoustic guitars and xylophones: it had to be Chesterfield. Despite my stage nerves, the effect was relaxing, like waterbeds and cups of mint tea.

'Hey, it even matches my outfit.' I slipped the ring on, easy-as. We exchanged a smile.

He cleared his throat. 'So Miss Mannix, I was wondering . . .'

Suddenly from over his shoulder, a shadow loomed and my insides turned to ice. The face moved into the light and it was indeed Justin, loose in a leather jacket, talking on a new release Nokia. My heart decided now was the time to take up javelin.

'. . . That is, if you're not busy.' Emil clicked loudly in front of my face. 'Earth to Mia, come in Mia.'

'Sorry, what?'

'Tomorrow night,' he repeated, in an 'I've totally just said this' way. 'At the observatory. Once in a lifetime chance to see Mars from a certain . . .'

'Yeah, sweet. I'm in.' *Justin was gone. Why were we talking about Mars?*

'Great! That's great! I know it sounds nerdy but it's actually pretty . . .'

'Sorry, Emil, I have to go. Band stuff . . .'

'Oh, okay,' he called after me. 'Good luck!'

'Cheers!' I called back over my shoulder. 'And thanks for the ring!'

Now or never, baby. I felt giddy-dopey, but as instructed, ready to follow Lexie's Law for Landing Lads.

Pulling my playsuit down to reveal non-existent cleavage, I exhaled once, hard, into my hand. My breath smelt like . . . breath. Whatever. Putting on my best sultry strut, I turned the corner breezily. He was a few paces ahead of me. I walked up to him . . . and right past him, catwalk confident. I kept walking. Um, wasn't ignoring him supposed to . . .

'Mia!'

Bingo bango, Jackson. I turned innocently. 'Oh, hi, Justin.' One hand on hip, one dangling, head cocked coyly, mouth shut. *Don't start the conversation. Let them pursue you.*

'If it isn't the girl who pushes people into pools.'

I gave him a look like, *That all you got?* (Excellent multi-use facial expression.)

Him: 'Smoke?'

Me: *Yuck.* 'Cool.'

I leant forward as he lit the cancer stick. The muffled strains of Chesterfield had set the mood to romantic, and I tried hard to avoid staring at him. Jeez Louise the boy's visage could sell everything from breakfast bars to funeral homes. Death definitely wouldn't be a drag if those hands were easing me into a casket. Easing me gently . . .

'So, you nervous?'

Answer questions with questions — that keeps conversation flowing. 'Why would I be nervous?'

He smiled. ''Cause you're about to play a show?'

I sucked down some poisonous cig. 'Am I?'

The smile faltered. 'Aren't you?'

'What did you think?'

The smile morphed into a WTF expression. 'I thought you were on next.'

Look bored. Sound bored. 'Well then,' I sighed. 'I guess we are.'

Scope out the room while you're still talking to them. Glancing over his shoulder, I threw a flirty wink and a 'hey' at an invisible hottie. He turned to see who was there – no one – and looked back to me, mystifed.

'You don't sound that psyched.' He flicked ash onto the concrete. 'I couldn't sleep before our first show. I was so freaked my hand shook for half the set.'

Be mysterious. Keep them guessing. 'Well, I have a secret cure for pre-show nerves.' I let my lips curl up into a saucy smile.

'Really?' he asked, blowing smoke up past my shoulder. 'What?'

'If I told you, it wouldn't be a secret, would it?' I dropped my cigarette between us and stepped forward onto it. I flashed a coy look from lowered lashes – another Lexie secret – and didn't step back.

'I guess not . . .' he murmured, staring at me in a combination of overt fascination and dumbfounded confusion. 'But maybe one day I'll find out.' Lifting his non-smoking hand, he let one thumb slide down my arm hanging loose at my side.

I closed my eyes, feeling light-headed, my skin prickling hotly at his touch. I could smell his leather jacket, his aftershave . . .

'Maybe you will,' I whispered.

'*Mia!*' The moment was shattered by a distraught Seb, racing down the corridor towards me.

'Kinda in the middle of something here, Seb . . .' I muttered, flashing Justin another lowered lash look of lust.

He grabbed my arm, voice strained and breathless. 'Houston, we have a major freakin' problem.'

12

Two queens hit the deck and the punks hooted with laughter. 'Strip!'

Lexie threw her head back and squealed with them. She stood up unsteadily, whipped her singlet off, and screamed again.

'Drink!' the punks slurred, tossing her an all-but-empty bottle of vodka, which she slammed back to yells of approval from The Boners. Finally seeing us standing speechless in the doorway, she squealed again.

'*Dudes!* This is my band!' She flung the bottle high in salute, the sudden movement causing her to tip sideways onto a floor thick with half-naked drunk punks, evidently in the middle of strip poker.

'She's wasted,' I said to Seb, stunned. 'She can't sing like that. She can barely stand up.'

'Like I said,' Seb was losing his cool, '*problem.*'

'Black coffee,' I thought aloud, desperately trying to grasp memories of what happened in the movies. 'A lie-down? A cold shower?'

Greasy Ponytail tapped me on the shoulder. 'You're on in five, guys.' He glanced at the half-naked Lex, rolling on the floor in hysterics, with obvious interest. 'If you need a hand getting your singer onstage . . .'

'We can handle it,' Seb snapped. He turned to me grimly. 'Showtime.'

'C'mon Lex, not everyone wants to see you in your underwear,' I said soothingly, trying in vain to slip the singlet back over her head as we waited at the side of stage

'Yisss they do,' she slurred, giggling and swaying tipsily out of my reach. 'Maybe I should shing *naked*.'

'No, no, no, no,' we chorused in a panic, barely managing to stop her undoing her bra.

As Chesterfield bowed, smiling graciously at their applause, Seb and I exchanged doomed looks.

'Maybe we should pull out,' he whispered urgently. 'Food poisoning. Bad prawns.'

I swallowed hard. 'Too late.' Lexie had already stumbled onstage, grabbing the microphone roughly from the long-haired singer in paisley.

'*Hello Shydney!*' she yelled. 'Are you ready to *party*!?'

Her words fell flat, prompting only baffled, scattered applause.

'Please tell me this isn't happening,' muttered Seb, wiping his brow feverishly. 'We're a *freak show*.'

But if Lexie was deterred, she didn't show it. 'C'mon!' She cried, pumping her fist in the air. 'I *shaid*, Are you ready to *party*? *Start cheering, you guys!*'

Whether the crowd obeyed because of her sheer bravado or the fact there was a blonde babe onstage clearly off her head, we didn't know. But cheer they did, so it seemed there was nothing for it.

As Seb and I skulked onstage, reality dawned and applause started to swell — oh, we *were* the band, that wasn't just a drunk chick with *Guitar Hero* delusions. I glanced at Seb and slung my guitar over my shoulder. He shrugged helplessly, holding his sticks up to count us in. 'One, two. One, two, three, four!' With everything we had, Fire Fire slammed into our first song.

What came next was *not* something we had prepared earlier.

A writhing Lexie missed her cue on the first verse and instead started to play her synth part again. I looked around to Seb, who was staring at her in confusion, with no choice but to keep playing the same beat. I followed suit — looking desperately towards an oblivious Lexie — but she had her eyes closed, lost in her own world of an endless synth riff.

'Start singing!' Seb yelled at me. 'NOW!'

Without thinking I whipped my head to the mic, and began singing Lexie's part. I knew it as well as she did, but my voice sounded nothing like Lex's deep sexy snarl — it was too sweet, too thin, it seemed to change all the meaning of the words.

On hearing my voice, her eyes flew open and for a second I could see her start getting into the song, before realising slowly it was she who was supposed to be on the mic. She picked it up from the chorus, but after the bridge the same thing happened, and I ended up singing the second verse as Lexie danced around onstage singing the back-up.

Finishing the song together, Lexie turned to grin at me, giving me a pleased thumbs up. I gaped at her in bewilderment — was she so toasted that she had no idea what was going on, or had it actually worked out? Did we actually sound good singing together?

Seb shrugged helplessly and counted us into the next song.

As soon as the last note faded, Seb threw his drumsticks down in disgust and stormed offstage. I threw an unsure smile to the crowd, and followed him as he blazed a path to the band room.

'I can't believe it,' he choked, running his fingers through his hair in distress. 'I can't *believe* her.'

'C'mon, Seb, it wasn't that bad . . .'

'No, it was worse, Mia,' Seb railed. 'That was *a joke.*'

'All right!' Lexie fell into the band room, throwing her arms around us, reeking of booze. 'We rocked! Awesome! *Rock'n'roll!*'

Seb pushed her arm away harshly. 'Get a grip Lexie. Your inebriation has annihilated this band.'

She stared at him, confused. 'What's your problem? That was killer!'

'Are you crazy?' yelled Seb. 'You missed half your cues. Mia did more singing than you!'

'Yeah, and it sounded great!' she exclaimed, rolling her eyes. 'Jeez, don't be such a control freak.'

'Oh yeah, playing like we rehearsed is really being a control freak.' Seb's voice smacked of angry sarcasm. 'I'm sorry, I thought that was *the point of rehearsal.*'

Lexie's defences were rocketing sky-high. 'Seb, can you chill out? It's called *improvisation.*'

'It's called *getting wasted and ruining our first show.*' Seb lost it. 'I'm sick of it. I'm sick of having to make excuses for your *pathetic* irresponsibility!'

Her eyes hardened. 'I'm not listening to that shiz. C'mon Mia.' She turned to grab my arm and I quickly stared at the ground. 'I said, *c'mon,* Mia.' She went to snatch at my arm again, but I didn't let her.

The atmosphere changed. We had broken character rules.

I always went with Lexie if she wanted and Seb was always the sensible one that fixed things and didn't get mad.

'Wow, Seb.' Lexie said icily. 'It really sounds like you have something to say to me. Are you gonna say it, or are you gonna be a *total boy* about it?'

'You wanna know what I'm talking about? Fine.' Seb enunciated each word with deadly precision. 'I'm talking about you always being late to rehearsal, about you not helping set up or pack up, and you being the last one to learn your parts. I'm talking about your need to be centre of attention 24/7. I'm talking about you ruining this band!'

'Yeah?' Her eyes flashed at him. 'Well, that's who I am and you need me. Deal with it.'

Seb laughed harshly. 'That's the best part, Lex. I won't have to anymore. There's no way we'll win this heat. After tonight, Fire Fire ceases to exist. I quit.'

I stood shell-shocked.

Lexie turned to me slowly. 'Is that what you think too?'

Panic struck me — confrontations are not my strength. 'Maybe we should all just calm down . . .'

She stepped towards me, hands squarely on hips. 'Is that what you think too?'

'No,' I lied. 'It's not.'

She sneered at me in contempt. 'You're such a pathetic coward.'

'Don't talk to her that way,' Seb snapped.

'I don't need you to stick up for me, Seb,' I snapped back.

'You guys are both such *cowards*!' Lexie screamed. '*I hate you.*'

'HEY!' Greasy Ponytail stood in the doorway. 'They're announcing the winner. Onstage, now!'

'If I can have your attention . . .' A music dork in a Battle of the Bands T-shirt tapped the microphone, attempting to quiet the rowdy crowd. 'First of all we'd like to thank all the bands for playing . . .'

The four bands were clustered on stage, all cool photo ops except for us. Lexie and Seb were the divorced movie star couple – everyone could see they hated each other, but they had to do it for the fans. I was their publicist, stuck between them so they didn't kill each other.

Glancing over to the wings, I spotted Justin and Emil. They both acknowledged me with a nod and a half-smile, ignorant of the other's presence. Seb clocked this with grim amusement.

'Reality versus fantasy,' he muttered. 'The reality is: this fire is out.'

Lexie rolled her eyes. 'What happened to your positive attitude, Sebastian?'

Seb looked at her evenly. 'I think you drank it.'

'And while, in a way, all these bands are winners,' the dork was saying. 'In a more specific way, only one band will compete at the State Final next week. The envelope please . . .'

. . . and for a moment everything else seemed to fall away – the people watching, the judges examining us, the other bands onstage, Justin, Emil, school, home, everything. Suddenly it was just me, Lexie and Seb, despite the drama, despite all the crap. I felt dizzy and there was no sound, no light, nothing except us . . .

'The winner is . . .'

Lexie and Seb instinctively grabbed a hand each . . .

'Fire Fire.'

The crowd cheered, wild and animalistic. Lexie jumped up and down, screaming, 'I knew it! I knew we'd win!'

Photo flashes burst over us. We won? I felt confused and weird and hot, like I had a fever, it couldn't sink in, I couldn't move.

'Innovative use of two contrasting singers,' the dork read out. 'Impressive standard of drumming, dynamic stage presence from all performers and unique song structures. Congratulations to Fire Fire.'

Someone clapped me on the back.

'You guys!' Lexie shook our shoulders. 'Don't you get it? We did it! We won!'

Seb looked at me and started laughing incredulously. We won. We were playing the State Final. WE WON!

Soundtrack: 'Like An Arrow', The Red Sun Band
Mood: Luv-struck

'Strawberries dipped in chocolate.' I put my guitar case carefully into the back seat as Seb worked on bundling up cables efficiently.

'Hot guys dipped in chocolate,' he replied.

I frowned. 'A thousand blue M&Ms in a glass.'

'A thousand hot guys, dipped in chocolate, in a blue glass.'

I laughed. '*Dingdingdingdingding!* You're now in charge of all backstage demands.' I grunted, lugging the heavy guitar amp towards the car. 'Why don't we have roadies to do this?' I whinged. 'My beautiful hands are blistering!'

Seb chuckled as he helped me shove the beast into the boot. 'Hey, I was thinking about the show.' He cleared his throat, looking a little uncomfortable. 'What do you think about, well, maybe we can play around in rehearsal with two singers. The judges seemed to think it sounded okay.' He glanced at me. 'What? Why are you looking like that?'

'Hey.'

We turned to see a bedraggled Lexie limply holding a mic stand. Silently she walked up to the car and began shoving it awkwardly into the boot. Halfway through she stopped and stumbled to the bushes. The graceful sound of a quick spew ensued.

'And that is what we call,' Seb began channelling David Attenborough, 'a drunk teenager in their natural habitat. Listen carefully to its mating call. Isn't that magnificent?'

The words 'never . . . drinking . . . again' came muffled from the shrubs, before she reappeared as if walking on very, very thin ice. 'What else we gotta do?'

Seb cleared his throat. 'Mind the car, Mia. I'm going to teach Lex the ancient art of packing up a drum kit with a Grade A hangover.' He extracted the mic stand from the boot, giving her an amused look. 'These usually belong to the venue.' And then to me: 'Don't make out with any groupies while we're gone.'

'What if they're really hot groupies?' I called after them.

'Save them for me,' he hollered back.

The sound of their footsteps faded and for the first time that night there was nothing. No crazy fighting, no booming speakers, no cheering crowds, no bands, no boys, just total peace and quiet in an empty car park.

Climbing up onto the bonnet of the car, I sighed and stretched back against the windshield to gaze up at the stars. The cool metal was smooth and comforting against my back. Crickets whirred and clicked, as planets light years away in deep, silent space twinkled at me. It was hard to believe they were the same stars I used to stare at for hours from our back porch in the Snowy — it seemed like so long ago. So much had happened . . . My eyes started closing as a wave of exhaustion washed over me . . .

'Mia.'

I jumped, almost falling off the bonnet in fright. Without acknowledging I was practically asleep on a car bonnet — where else? — Justin handed me a flyer. 'Cool show. Come see my heat tomorrow night.'

Only someone that unnaturally attractive could get away with making an invitation a statement, not a request.

'Sure, if I can watch backstage,' I shot back cheekily.

He grinned at me. 'Your name's on the door. You can bring the band,' he offered, as he started strolling off into the darkness. 'But I really only want you.'

As lust flowed through me like molten lava, I looked at the flyer. Four brooding boys stood calmly in the middle of a snowfield filled with winged reindeer. Suddenly, anything was possible.

13

'*Merde!*' I slammed my locker in annoyance.

'What's wrong?' Charlie — the semi-famous chick whose locker was next to mine — asked in concern.

'I forgot my French textbook again,' I groaned, picturing it on my bedroom floor. 'Ms Tautou is gonna kill me . . .'

'Take mine,' she smiled, handing it over.

'But, won't you need . . .'

'Great show last night!' she called over her shoulder as she sailed off. '*Au revoir!*'

'Thanks — I mean, *merci!*'

'Hi, Mia.' A couple of unfamiliar dancing students gave me little waves as they floated past. Weird. That had been happening all morning . . .

'Mia!' Michael and Sarah from art class ran up, falling in step on either side of me. 'How's it going?'

'It's going fine,' I answered suspiciously. 'What's up?'

Michael pulled an invitation out of his pocket. 'Having a party this weekend. Be awesome if you guys could play.'

'This weekend, as in the day after tomorrow?' I asked, inspecting the hand-written invite. 'Bit late to plan a party, isn't it?'

'Oh, the party's been planned for ages—,' he started, a swift kick from Sarah cutting him off.

'But I wasn't invited,' I finished for him. 'Until now.'

'Well, I didn't think your band would be so good.' Cue a second kick.

I shoved the flyer in my bag, repeating the mantra I'd been busting out all morning. 'Thanks for the offer, but I'll have to ask the band.'

It didn't end there. Kids who'd previously ignored me started arguing over sitting next to me in class. Every joke I made was hilarious. Someone offered to make us a video clip. I was invited to three more parties. Were these overtures of friendship real, or would they fade just as quickly if we bombed at the Final? Maybe we were the equivalent of the canteen's sticky date pudding: today's special, until someone landed a feature film role tomorrow and became the school's apple crumble.

'Cheers,' I said, as the pudding plopped on my tray. 'How much do I owe you?'

The rosy-cheeked canteen lady smiled at me knowingly. 'Rock stars eat on the house today.'

I shuddered, and not just because I'd heard an old person say 'rock stars'. 'This is crazy,' I muttered to myself. 'Who makes one win such a big deal?'

'Mia, baby!' And everything abruptly fell into place. Whereas my post-gig outfit consisted of jeans and a second-hand cowgirl shirt, Lexie wouldn't have looked out of place at a trashy Fashion Week afterparty (i.e. any of them). Teaming pink tights and bangles with the pink flamingo wig, she was wearing a very strange, angular dress that looked like she'd pinned a few metres of black taffeta around herself after rolling out of bed at the crack of midday.

'That's exactly what I did!' she exclaimed when I pointed this out. 'Isn't it fabulous?'

'Hey, Lex, Mia!' a couple of randoms yelled to us.

'Let's party on the weekend, babies!' she called back, blowing them kisses.

'Who were they?' I asked.

'No idea.' She scarfed some pudding from my tray. 'I've been having the best day! Walk me to the front of school?'

'Hey guys, see you at the party then!' Michael called as we walked through the schoolground.

'Love you like a rock star, babe!' she shouted back with a wave.

'We're playing that party?' I asked. 'Did you ask Seb?'

'Who cares?' she shrugged. 'If we don't show up, it's even cooler.'

'Speaking of showing up,' I remembered. 'Justin's Battle of the Bands heat is on tonight. Wanna come with?'

'Actually,' she smiled secretively, as we reached the front of school, 'I have plans.'

'Plans?' I asked. 'What plans . . .'

My question was drowned out by a car with a cruddy motor rattling to the front of the school, pumping out hardcore punk. Crammed inside were The Boners, plus entourage.

'Guys!' Lexie waved happily.

'What about English?' I yelled as she raced to the car. 'We've got a test today!'

'I'm a rock star, babe!' she yelled back, hopping into the front seat. 'And stars only come out at night!'

I shook my head in disbelief as the car roared off. Only Lexie would take being a star to such extremes . . . Well, this star couldn't just come out at night, this star . . .

'Stars,' I thought aloud. 'Oh no. *Stars!*'

Spinning on my heel, I raced back into school.

'Hello?' I pushed Emil's office door open gingerly. 'Emil?'

Opening the door fully, I came face-to-face with a life-size cardboard cut-out of Bill Murray in *Ghostbusters*, Proton Pack at the ready.

Oh-kay, I thought to myself. Someone's been spending way too much time on eBay.

I picked up a sleepy Libby for a cuddle, looking around the empty office for more clues as to the Ghostbuster's presence. My eye was drawn to a bright red briefcase on Emil's desk. Looking closer I noticed *Alien Survival Kit* was written on it in his telltale scrawl. Feeling only slightly snoopy, I clicked it open.

Inside were all manner of ghost-and-ghoul memorabilia: a kitschy 1950s 'ghost trap' was packed next to two pairs of see-in-the-dark binoculars while a pocket-sized novelty phrasebook containing 'Hello and welcome' in a billion different languages was tucked next to DVDs of *ET*, *Star Wars* and, of course, *Ghostbusters*.

'That was supposed to be a surprise, McSnoopy,' Emil remarked, appearing in the doorway with a bag full of picnic food.

'Well colour me surprised!' I quipped. 'Is this all for tonight?'

He feigned shock. 'Don't believe the hype — people's memories actually *improve* with age!'

'Shut up,' I laughed weakly. 'Of course I remembered.'

He dumped the food on his desk, a slight edge grazing his tone. 'I can't see dead people but my sixth sense is definitely picking up a "but" . . .'

I smiled in a way I hoped was 'charming'. 'How do you feel about *two* types of stargazing tonight?'

Soundtrack: 'Get Out, Give In', Expatriate
Mood: Obsessed

While Silver Street's Battle of the Bands heat had been packed with a cross-section of kids from the arty end of the spectrum, the exclusive Prince's College had a considerably narrower focus.

'Gorgeous private school guys,' Seb announced, as we waited for Emil out the front of their school concert hall. 'And tons of them. Pinch me, Mia. I've died and gone to heaven.'

'I still think Justin's the hottest one, don't you?' I stretched up on my toes, scanning the crowd intently. 'I think it's the scowl. Or maybe the smirk, I can't tell . . .'

'And today's meeting of the Justin Jackson Fan Club will now come to a close.' His look was low-key concern. 'Doesn't it strike you as odd you're taking the guy who likes you to see the guy you like play a show? That's such a twisted date, if I didn't know better, I'd swear I was with Lexie.'

'It's not a date,' I snapped defensively. 'We're hanging out. No expectations – with anyone.'

He held his hands up in surrender. 'Whatever you say, Paris Hilton. But you know what they say about playing with fire . . .'

'Hey Seb. Hi Mia.' Emil appeared at our side, clutching the Alien Survival Kit and handing me a white rose. 'Yeah, supposedly there's a tradition with flowers and dates . . .'

'Mia!' Justin winked at me from across the crowded entrance. 'See you inside.'

' . . . Something about getting burned.' Seb shrugged.

'Name?' The clipboard-wielding woman at the door enquired officiously.

'Mia Mannix.' *Mia Jackson*, I thought to myself absent-mindedly as she inspected the guest list carefully. *Doesn't sound too shabby at all.*

'Mia Mannix, Seb Vardakas and Lexie Cannon, from Silver Street High?'

'Yep, but Lexie isn't coming so can I bring him instead?' I gestured to Emil.

The woman tutted. 'We can't change names on the guest list.'

'But . . .'

'No excuses.' She shook her head vehemently. 'Your names are already printed on the backstage passes.'

'Oh.' I could hear the first band start playing inside the hall and FOMO reared its ugly head. Fear Of Missing Out. I turned back to Emil awkwardly. 'Well, then, maybe I can meet you later, after the gig?'

Emil blinked, like he'd just heard a gunshot, before stuttering, 'Oh, sure. No worries.'

Seb's stare couldn't have been frostier if I'd suggested we skip the gig to watch homeless people fistfight. He strode up to the woman with the clipboard and in his best 'don't you know who I think I am' voice said: 'I'm in the band that won Silver Street High's heat last night and *this* is our manager, Emil.'

The woman's eyebrows went skyhigh, calling his bluff.

Seb matched her brow for brow. 'Emil *Allen*. Wunderkind of the music industry?' He leaned forward, voice dropping to a conspiratorial whisper. 'The last three bands he signed all went top ten, *plus* he manages three *Idol* finalists. You have to keep this under wraps but he's here tonight *to sign a new act.*'

'Well, I suppose for *industry guests*, we can *massage* the rules.' She shark-smiled creepily as she handed over the backstage passes. 'Enjoy the show. Oh, and Emil? Watch out for The Devil's Dirty Death Squad.' Proud mum smile. 'That's my son's band.'

'Are you kidding me? These guys are totally derivative!' I exclaimed to Kien. 'It's like, "Hey guys, early eighties post-punk called and they want all their songs back".'

'I'm with Mia,' Trick shrugged. 'Okay, we weren't alive then but that's no excuse for ripping off Joy Division . . .'

'That last song? Totally Gang of Four,' I continued airily. 'I feel like I'm back in the age of VHS and ra-ra skirts.'

As the boys chuckled their agreement, I sighed happily. Is there anything better than chewing the fat backstage with two cool rock boys, when you yourself are a certified cool rock chick? No, there is not. The band in question, Ninja Wolf School, finished to loud applause and high-pitched cheers from the pack of eager girls crowding the front of the stage. They shuffled offstage, and Trick and Kien slapped them lazy high-fives in a mumbled montage of 'cool show, dude' and 'awesome, man'.

'Hey, Mannix,' Seb appeared smartly at my shoulder. 'What's the 411?'

'Seb, where've you been?' As I spun around I noticed a familiar shadow slouched against a wall behind him. My heart jumped up and down in excitement and then I started to feel a bit sick.

Justin was gazing at me intently.

'Hanging with Emil,' Seb replied, a tad touchy.

I nodded, letting my eyes flick back to Justin for a beat. 'This is Trick and Kien, they play in The Alaska Family.'

'Hey, man.' Kien shook Seb's hand warmly.

'Jackson says you're a mad-awesome drummer,' Trick added.

'Yes, I am both awesome and mad,' Seb replied calmly.

'Mia, we're going to get some fresh air before these guys play. Would you like to join us?'

'I, um . . . I need to . . .' Past Seb's shoulder, I could see Justin's lips curl into a late night smirk, a pin-up smile, an amused scowl. How is it possible for one person to be so damn sexy? I wanted badly to hear his low, throaty voice muttering illicit desires in my ear . . .

'Bathroom,' I blurted out, flushed. 'I gotta powder my nose.'

Seb ran his hand through his hair, seemingly agitated. 'Fine. Come outside when you're done. Nice meeting you guys.'

As Trick and Kien melted off to start setting up, I watched Seb stalk back to Emil, seated uncomfortably on some fold-up plastic chairs near the exit. I felt a pang of guilt. Maybe I should forget about Justin and go hang out with . . .

'Boyfriend?'

I jumped. 'Jeez, what is it with you and the sneak-up? Someone needs to get you some very squeaky unsneaky shoes.'

Justin nodded at Emil, eyes dark and impenetrable. 'So, is the nerdling your boyfriend?'

I opened my mouth to confirm that *no, no way, no how*, as Lexie's instructions suddenly sashayed back to me: *Designer, not 7/11*. Time to bust out some foolproof femme fatale moves.

1. Tipping my head to the side, I thought about the question, repeating it to myself in low-key amusement, 'Is he my *boyfriend* . . .'
2. I smiled at some very delicious secret memory.
3. Finally breaking my daydream, I looked back to an attentive Justin. 'No. Not really . . .'

'Not really?' Hook, line and sinker. 'What does that mean?'

I flashed him Lexie's patented I've-got-a-million-naughty-secrets-up-my-sleeve look, before stepping past him en route to the exit. 'Have a good show, Justin.'

Breezing outside, I felt like the cat who swallowed the canary, eager to recount my success to Seb.

'Yo, Sebola, where's Emil?'

'Waiting for you,' he replied. 'Why are you —'

'You will not bee-leeeave what just happened between me and Justin,' I began dramatically, 'Okay, so he asks me . . .'

'You were with Justin just now?'

'Justin just now,' I repeated. 'Hey, that sounds like a good song name . . .'

Seb grabbed my shoulders. 'Mia, what is wrong with you?'

'Huh?' I shook his hands off, irritated. 'What's wrong with *you*?'

'Look,' Seb breathed out carefully. 'I get that this guy is the dreamiest dreamboat to ever set sail in your harbour. But you've gotta do the right thing by Emil.'

'What about Emil?' I asked, mystified. 'We got him in, didn't we?'

'*I* got him in, Mia. He's your date and he's spending more time with me!'

'I'm not ignoring him!' I exclaimed. 'I mean, we're just friends . . .'

'If that's the way you treat your friends, I must be crazy to call you mine,' Seb looked at me with that incredibly annoying mixture of concern and disappointment. 'I'm really surprised you'd do this to someone after . . .'

My eyes flew to meet his. 'After what?'

'After . . .' He back-pedalled awkwardly.

'After starting at Silver Street as a friendless freak?' I spat.

'After being the girl no one wanted to talk to? I'm not apologising for finally winning some respect from people. Just because I'm here with someone who's not as popular as me doesn't mean I have to babysit them!'

I turned around and pushed my way inside, head spinning wildly. My word-vomit had left a bad taste in my mouth and with every step that took me to the backstage entrance, I wished more and more I could take it back. Why was I getting so defensive? Maybe because Seb was right — I should find Emil.

But as I sunk against a back wall, dazed, watching everyone chat and flirt and laugh like normal people, I realised Emil might not want to talk to *me*. Which sucked, because I really felt like someone to spill to about everything, and, ironically, Emil was usually my go-to guy. Good one, Mannix.

'I'm an idiot,' I moaned to myself.

'Ah, that explains the drool and the court jester hat, then.'

'Hey, Emil,' I smiled weakly, as he came to lean next to me. 'Sorry I've been so . . . distracted.'

'Do you like Justin?' he asked lightly. 'It's fine if you do. I just need to know.'

'Do I like . . . Justin?' Uh-oh. This wasn't good.

'Hey, if I was a girl, *I'd* probably like Justin,' he joked. 'The appeal is pretty obvious.'

Emil looked so damn sweet and sad and lo-fi sexy standing there, half in shadows, glancing cautiously down at me, I found myself leaning up to brush his cheek with a quick kiss. 'Justin and I — we're friends. I'm here with you, aren't I?'

He exhaled in relief. 'Cool.'

The lights dimmed as The Alaska Family traipsed onstage to crowd-favourite applause and the obligatory chorus of wolf-whistles. As everyone else's eyes locked on The Simultaneous Source Of My Life's Happiness And Grief establishing himself as front man extraordinaire, mine were desperately sweeping the backstage area for a shovel to dig myself out of the hole I'd put myself in.

'No surprises there,' Emil commented, after the guys shuffled past us on the way to post-victory adulation. 'What did you think?'

'Some of their songs are little too "pub rock" for me,' I admitted. 'But they have great stage presence.'

'Well, I *know* you're an expert on great stage presence,' Emil replied teasingly. 'But how are you with constellations?'

'Dude, I could pick the saucepan out when I was four!' I said in mock-outrage, sticking him in the ribs. 'Just try me . . .'

'Hey, guys.' Our laughter was stopped short by guess who.

'Hey man, congratulations,' Emil offered diplomatically, but I could tell Justin had put him on edge.

'Thanks.' Justin's eyes drilled into me powerfully. 'So State Finals, huh? You ready for the competition?'

I smiled coolly. 'Bring it on, Jackson.'

Sweat slicked his brow: sexy, masculine. 'Stick round for the afterparty.' He handed me an address.

'Thanks but we've got plans,' Emil replied testily.

'Actually I was only inviting her,' Justin smiled briefly at Emil. 'Sorry man — it's a friends only thing.'

As Justin tore his eyes away from me and began making for the door, I swallowed nervously. Had Emil noticed how charged the air between me and Justin had just been?

He exhaled with anger. 'Man, I don't wanna diss on

your friends or anything but Justin makes Tom Cruise look humble. Let's split.'

Sweet Gyllenhaal, I couldn't move. I desperately willed myself to put one foot in front of the other and follow Emil — my friend, who I really liked and respected and didn't want to hurt at all, *not at all* — but I couldn't. It was like Justin was a magnet and whether I liked it or not, I was bound to him and the promise of what could happen between us; thoughts that had been flooding my mind since we'd met. Tonight was the night, I knew it.

When he realised I wasn't in step beside him, Emil turned back curiously. 'C'mon,' he smiled. 'It's getting late.'

I stared at him, wracked with guilt. 'I'm sorry,' I whispered.

'What for? Mia, what's wrong?'

I stared at my shoes: Lexie's shiny red kitten heels — seduction in a shoe, she'd promised. Now it'd be heartbreak in a heel.

'I want to stay.'

The truth broke across Emil's face like a thunderclap. 'You want to stay because you've stepped in superglue and you're stuck to the floor, or you want to stay because . . . of him?'

My eyes stung with tears as I squeezed his arm. 'Emil, I'm sorry, you probably hate me now . . .'

Pulling his arm away from mine slowly, he took a step back, assessing me as it all made sense. He started nodding and shaking his head at the same time, a pained smile twisting at his mouth.

'Well, Mia. You can add another achievement to your tally. Made new friends, started a band and taken someone on the most humiliating date of their life.'

And then he turned and walked away.

Soundtrack: 'Raised By Wolves',
Midnight Juggernauts
Mood: Over it

If TV has taught me anything, it's that love conquers all, drugs are bad, and rock'n'roll afterparties always involve tons of hot people having ridiculous amounts of fun. Usually this movie montage involves sexed-up d-floor action undertaken by you and your crew (all sporting awesome outfits), hilarious yet insightful conversations with complete strangers, platters of colourful gourmet food served with a wink and a nod by cute waiters and a selection of free-flowing substances that definitely aren't part of a family friendly prime-time slot. This soiree had all of the above in spades, so why was I feeling so damn miserable?

'Maybe because you broke a really nice guy's heart for someone who's been ignoring you all night?' Seb suggested, sipping a fruity concoction perfunctorily.

'Save it, Vardakas,' I muttered, watching Justin flirt casually with everyone but me. 'I get it. I screwed up.'

'You truthenised,' he shrugged. 'It has consequences.'

'I truth-a-what-now?'

'Truthenise. To inform someone of a truth that leaves them impotent and powerless,' he grinned, self-satisfied. 'Get it? Like euthanise . . .'

'Yeah, I get it,' I interrupted icily. 'Way to make me feel better, moron.'

141

'I'm gonna go mingle,' Seb pouted. 'You wanna be on your own anyway, right? Why else would you dump your would-be boyfriend for a no-chance-in-hell boyfriend?'

I narrowed my eyes at him as he fled smugly. It was time to split. This had turned into a night for sad folk songs and some serious ceiling staring.

Picking my way past the weird, the wonderful and the wasted, I noticed a flyer for a band called What's the Occasion? Alien Invasion! sticking out of a rubbish bin. I fished it out, wondering if Emil was stargazing without me. And the Award for the Screw-Up of the Year goes to:

'Mia. Why are you going through the trash?'

To find my dignity, I answered silently. 'Great party, Justin, but I'm gonna bail.'

He grabbed my arm as I pushed past him. 'You're leaving? So soon?'

I pulled it back, annoyed. 'Deal with it.'

'But we haven't had a chance to hang . . .'

'That's what happens when you ignore someone all night.'

'Hey!' He threw his hands up in mock-protest. 'I come in peace. C'mon. I'll get you a drink.'

Flashing on Lexie throwing her guts up in the bushes, I shook my head, suddenly exhausted. 'I'm just gonna go.'

He shrugged, the physical manifestation of the phrase 'whatever'. 'I'll walk you out.'

'I don't know why you need a key to let me out . . . oh. Wow.'

Speechless, I followed Justin through the door he'd just unlocked to a private viewing booth overlooking the stage at the back of the hall.

'I thought they only had these at football games and the opera,' I murmured, taking in the sumptuous velvet-edged chairs, old fashioned lamps and gorgeous chaise lounge. It was like something out of *Moulin Rouge*: decadent and secret.

'Pretty nice, huh?' He stared down at the party in full swing beneath us. 'Sometimes I like to get away from everything.'

'Tired of playing "sought-after rock star"?' I asked, sinking into the soft lounge. 'Oh, what a hard life you lead.'

He glanced at me in surprise. 'You've got quite a mouth on you, Mannix. So, what's this about me ignoring you?'

'Call me crazy but when you invite someone to hang out, it generally means you actually hang out with them.' I folded my arms, a smile spreading across my face. It's fun teasing boys. They're such easy targets.

'Okay.' He turned round to face me, eyes drinking me in slowly. 'Maybe you should teach me better manners.'

A quick thrill ran through me but I feigned nonchalance, hoping the low lighting would disguise the crimson blush that wasn't make-up. 'First, you should've found me and said hello.'

He sank down onto the couch, one arm resting along the back, only inches from mine.

'Hello, Mia.' Cue trademark smirk.

'And then you should say something nice to me.'

He let his eyes trail up and down before finally meeting mine. In this light, they looked almost black. A line from a science textbook hovered over him: 'A black hole is an object with a gravitational field so powerful, that light itself cannot escape its pull.' Science, it seemed, was right.

In a low and husky voice he said simply, 'I've wanted you since the moment I saw you, that day in the record store.'

I froze, involuntarily holding my breath. Slowly he stretched out his hand, sliding his fingers towards mine and all of a sudden they were interlaced.

'C'mere.' Pulling me towards him he wrapped my arms around his neck, my body fitting into his perfectly, close, warm. He ran his fingers down my back, my arms, my fingers – his hands big and strong as they rubbed my skin. I closed my eyes, and my fingers found their way into his unwashed hair, down his cheek until his lips caught them in a kiss, sucking on their tips.

I breathed in his smell: a warm, spicy aftershave as dark as the night itself. He leaned towards me but I pulled back so his lips tickled my cheek instead.

'Isn't this the part where someone runs in and interrupts us?' I murmured, looking to the doorway.

He tipped my face towards his. 'Not this time.'

He kissed me. Soft quick kisses at first, which fast became more and more urgent, desperate, driving. Every fantasy I'd had about this moment was suddenly playing out in high def and surround sound.

In no time we were spread out on the couch, me on top of him, his hands running through my hair, down my body, pushing my hips against his. I was breathless and it was primal, animalistic.

I was groaning, I think he was too. and then somehow he was on top of me, his whole heavy body pressed against mine, my eyes shut as he kissed me again and again and again.

'You're hot,' he whispered deep in my ear. 'I want you so bad.' Slowly, he began unbuttoning my shirt.

My eyes locked into his as he flipped the material open, revealing the semi-decent bra I'd thankfully remembered to wear. His fingers snuck up under the tight white lace, making me giddy, and burning up.

Slowly, his eyes still trained on mine, his fingers started moving south, gliding over the soft mound of my stomach and down to the top of my skirt and underwear. Then his fingers slipped underneath until . . . until . . .

'Until what?' Lexie and Seb exclaimed in breathless unison.

'Until I told him we should stop and he dropped me home,' I finished with a grin.

They both screamed and fell back on my bed. Needless to say, my tell-all account of the saucy soiree with my (former) Untouchable Crush had gone down quite a treat.

'I *so* thought you were gonna do it!' Lexie moaned. 'Why didn't you do it!?'

'Are you crazy?' I lay flat on my stomach and started flicking through magazines. 'That was my first hook-up with anyone *ever*!'

'Oh yeah, it'd be awful,' she realised. 'Dude, fool around more.'

'I plan on it. We're going out tonight.'

'Sweet!' We high-fived. 'Now, I'm just gonna get some more fabric samples from my car . . .'

'*More* fabric samples?' The boy and I chorused in alarm. We were surrounded by piles of new drawings, mountains of fabric swatches and stacks of sizes to play with: planning our costumes for the State Final had been well underway when Seb had finally asked how my night ended up.

'Yu-huh. Deal with it.'

As she clomped down the stairs I glanced at Seb self-righteously, and dramatically cleared my throat. 'So, contrary to popular belief, it happened. Oh, I've been looking forward to saying this: I. Told. You . . .'

'Slow down, Little Miss Frisky,' Seb interrupted, fingering the emerald-green material I'd decided on for a dress. 'You haven't won this race yet. You've barely started.'

'Ex-squeeze me?' I gaped in disbelief. 'Have you not been listening to my tell-all account of—'

'A hot hook-up, does not a relationship make,' Seb explained calmly. Then as a muttered afterthought: 'I, of all people, know this to be true . . .'

'What's that supposed to mean?'

He grabbed my guitar and began strumming chords idly; a classic Sooky-Seb-doesn't-wanna-talk-about-important-stuff move. 'Nothing. Let's keep working out costumes . . .'

I put my hand flat over the strings. 'Babysugarhoney. It's me, remember? The person you tell things to.'

He sighed and pulled a face. 'Oh, you know . . . Just be grateful you have options . . .'

I frowned. 'Enough with the cryptic crossword clues Sherlock. What's the deal?'

He put the guitar down. 'Three letters. A sexual orientation that while beneficial for an above-average dress sense and emotional sensitivity, does not guarantee a romance-filled teen experience.'

I sat back against the fabric piles, as the sudden realisation hit me: I was living in a *you*niverse, population: me. Out of all the hours we'd spent discussing my love-life, I'd never once asked about Seb's.

'But there are queer guys at school, I just thought you weren't interested in a boyfriend.'

'There are five guys playing for my team at school and trust me, none of them are boyfriend-worthy,' Seb informed me.

'Well, I love you,' I said honestly. 'And if the boys here don't realise how amazing you are, then I guess you'll have to accept that patience is a virtue.'

He sighed dejectedly. 'That is the most depressing and unfair thing in the history of the world.'

15

'That'll be Lex!' I hollered to Dad, as Justin honked his horn
for a second ear-splitting time. Grabbing desperately at
some plastic black beads, I raced to the bathroom to check
my much-deliberated-on outfit — neon yellow singlet, black
bubble skirt and cute ankle boots — was still up to scratch. As
Justin leaned on his horn for a third time, I realised I hated
everything I was wearing, but too late now. Thundering
down the stairs, checking I had phone, lip-gloss (for some
reason, three different tubes) and keys, I bowled straight
into Dad, on his way up to find me.

'Sorry!' Words rushed, out of breath. 'My fault! I'm late!'

Dad was a picture of suspicion. 'You're very dressed up for
a movie, pet.'

'Are you kidding?' I replied dismissively, inching towards
the front door. 'The cinema is the new nightclub. You should
see what the other kids wear.'

Dad peeked through the blinds. 'Did Lexie get a
new car?'

My hand reached for the knob, willing a speedy exit.
'Yeah, her mum buys her a new one, like, every week. More
money than sense, huh?' I attempted a chuckle. 'Well, I'll see
you later . . .'

Dad took off his spectacles and wiped them thoughtfully.
'Maybe I've been too harsh on Lexie. She's important to you,
so she's important to me. I should come out and say hello.'

'No! No, you can't!' I babbled, standing in his path. 'Look, the truth is I'm dating the hottest rock star in town and he's in that car. You can't come and say hello because *I would die*.'

Dad stared at me in amazement as my confession sank in. I'm pretty sure the fact we hadn't had the can-I-date conversation meant the can-I-get-into-a-souped-up-mustang-with-a-ridiculously-good-looking-musician conversation was *not* going to go well. What in Jake's name had I done?

'Oh, Mia, what an imagination you have.' He smiled fondly. 'I'll get to know Lexie another time. Have a nice night.'

A usual Saturday night in the life of Mia Mannix went something like this: Fire Fire finish rehearsal around seven (after Lexie pretends to faint from exhaustion, dehydration or both); we head to Dimitri's Pizzeria to order vegetarian pizza and perve on passers-by; pound the pavement as Lexie plans an overly complex and inevitably ill-fated attempt to sneak into a club, bar or gig; rent DVDs; drive to mine; raid fridge for Vanilla Fudge Brownie ice-cream and scoff until we all feel sick.

Tonight, however, was shaping up to be a little different. For starters, I was on a date. A real date, with a real potential boyfriend. This was a first in the chronicles of Mia Mannix.

'I thought we'd head to Baby, see what's happening,' Justin was saying, overtaking with carefree abandon. Fast-food wrappers and slurpee cups nestled at my feet. I ensured my posture was correct (as per Seb's first date checklist): Shoulders back and relaxed, back straight, boobs out.

'Sophisticated yet understated.' I nodded thoughtfully. 'I love Baby.'

'You know it?' he asked, glancing at his reflection in the rear-view mirror.

'Um, no,' I admitted, laughing.

As we pulled up to a red light, he leaned over and unexpectedly pashed me, slippery lips salty like french fries. Pulling back, he squeezed my hand. 'You don't have to lie to get me to like you, babe.'

I hadn't heard of Baby but apparently the hot and the happening had. Immaculately manicured feet strapped into impossibly high heels stubbed out cig butts impatiently, in a line that stretched around the corner from the low-key red neon sign guarded by extras from *The Sopranos*.

'I don't mind queuing,' I informed Justin as we crossed the busy road. 'It'll give us a chance to talk.'

'You queue at a bank,' he stated, striding past those who were. 'Not when you're partying.' As the bouncer slapped him on the back in recognition, he leaned into my ear. 'Talking is also optional'. His hand found my bum as he followed me down the steps and into the club.

Soundtrack: 'I'm What You Need', Pomomofo
Mood: Ready for anything

Baby: A small but select pack of liquored up, rock'n'roll ready tan-fastic hotties, slithering like snakes to slippery electro. Tiny goldfish swam in an aquarium that spanned the wall behind the busy bar, oblivious to the social jungle just beyond their reach. Old televisions playing a surreal black-and-white film occupied random corners, while lights like exploding stars hung low. Everything was silver or neon and surface, just surface.

Justin was evidently a regular, unable to take five steps without being showered with recognition.

'You own this place?' I joked, after the fifth person had

yelled 'Dude!' or 'Babe!' in his general direction and been rewarded with a 'Wassup?' or knocked knuckles.

'Will one day,' he replied. 'It's my parent's. Oh hey, Louis!' He waved over a laid-back blond kid wielding a large camera, and slung his arm around my shoulders as a flash popped, blinding me.

'Huh?' I blinked.

Louis whipped out a small pad. 'Name?'

'Mia Mannix,' Justin replied for me, grabbing Louis's camera and scrolling back to see the photo. 'Mannix — with an x.'

'Ah,' Louis nodded, smiling. 'The painter's daughter. Very cool. Later, man.'

'Wait — what just happened?' I asked, as Louis ambled off to keep snapping.

'Social photos, baby,' he replied, with a grin. 'You gotta give people something to aspire to. Plus you look so cool, it'd be a crime not to print the proof.'

'Are you saying I'm a photo op?' I replied, bemused. 'Isn't that a little tasteless?'

He laughed as though I was making a joke. 'I'll get drinks.'

Seb and Lexie guaranteed me five here's-one-we-prepared-earlier conversation starters would be enough to see me through my night on the town. But after flying through his opinions of Facebook ('I just joined the group "I judge people who don't use iPods"'), The Alaska Family ('hard work but, like, awesome'), what his parents did ('make money and fight') and Prince's College ('full of rich jerks and wanker coke dealers — and that's just my friends') in a record fifteen minutes, I was down to my fifth and final topic. According to Seb's PowerPoint presentation, this topic should be introduced many hours into our night, at the height of deliciously devilish flirtation, and would seal the deal, f'real. Right now, I wasn't so sure, but I had nothing else up my sleeve.

Me: smiling playfully, 'So . . . if you could take five things to a desert island, would I be one of them?

He: a double take. '*What?*'

'I said, 'If you could take . . .'

'I heard the question.' He fingered his collar, giving me a weird look. 'I just don't really get it. You want me to take you to a desert island?'

'Forget it.' I smiled feebly. 'Dumb question.'

He took a long slug of Coke and JD. 'You're weird.'

'Sorry.' I muttered, wanting badly to disappear into the coffee-coloured leather sofa we were nestled in.

'No,' he said slowly. 'It's . . . interesting.'

Experimental films are interesting. The fact Australia is the only country in the world where we eat the animals on our coat of arms – that's kind of interesting. First dates are meant to be the social equivalents of caramel-flavoured moccacinos: sweet, frothy and fun, not 'interesting'. Why was maintaining a basic conversation with Justin so hard? We were *into* each other. If Emil was here we'd be off and racing on some kind of ridiculous conversation about our plans for life on a desert island, bantering over which new coffee flavours our Starbucks franchise would be offering: Wild Coconut Cappuccino versus Poison Berry Frappe. I smiled wistfully and then abruptly caught myself. Why was Emil making a cameo in my subconscious? The guy I wanted – Justin – was right next to me. I confirmed this fact by shifting half an inch closer to him, the sides of our knees grazing like stray icebergs.

A couple of dudes skulked by in backwards caps and baseball shirts – Australiana Americana – throwing Justin a 'Hey bro' and checking me out.

'What do you reckon people think of us?' Justin suddenly asked. 'Y'know – as a couple.'

It was my turn for jaw droppage. 'I . . . don't know. I have no idea.' What did people think of us? What did that mean? How could I possibly know that? What did *he* think of us as a couple? I felt panic bubble up through me: insecurity overload. The shortening of breath and look of raw alarm must've been obvious even in our shadowy corner.

'Hey,' he cupped my cheek in his hand, 'don't freak. Sometimes, I totally don't think before I talk. I really dig you, you know?'

'I like you too, Justin,' I replied, smooth as I could. 'You're really . . . *interesting*.'

He chuckled, back in character. 'Oh man, one date and she's already giving it to me.'

Channelling Lex, I whispered something wicked in his ear.

'Now that,' he murmured, 'is definitely interesting . . .'

'*Excuse me!*'

Woah. Major needle scratching off a record. A glowering Nikki Moretti towered over us, her sheer red dress leaving very little to anyone's imagination – especially a teenage guy's.

'Can I borrow my date for a minute?' she asked me, eyes flashing deliberately.

I blinked. 'Actually Moretti, Justin's *my* date.'

She smiled sweetly. 'Not for much longer. *Now*, Jackson.'

Justin groaned. 'Nik, I'm not up for the crazy psycho thing . . .'

'But it's *important*.' Her snarl relaxed into a lash-lowered pout, big eyes threatening to fill with hot tears. 'Juzzy . . .'

'Fine,' he mumbled. 'This better be good . . .'

'Justin!' I choked.

'I'll be back,' he called over his shoulder, as Nikki marched him off, all angry, sassy sexiness. Staring at the melting ice-cubes in my untouched drink, I felt exactly five years old, and completely out of my element.

Outside, the line had dwindled to a quarter of its size. I gulped in fresh night air, leaning against the scratchy brick wall, overwhelmed. Maybe I wasn't ready for a lead singer boyfriend. Rock royalty Courtney Love had it pretty tough – the week before her band's breakthrough album was released, hubbie Kurt Cobain goes and commits suicide. Courtney's cool: sure, she's a walking narcotics unit these days, but when she was my age she read a Sylvia Plath poem to audition for the Mickey Mouse Club. Sylvia wrote one of my favourite books, *The Bell Jar*, and then killed herself by putting her head in an oven. Why are all artists so weird and doomed?

Dad didn't seem any weirder than most clueless adults, but then, I had nothing to compare him to. He's always been like that, just like – and I don't even know why the thought unexpectedly popped into my head – just like my mum has always been dead. I never even knew her, so I can't miss a proper memory of her – like, 'oh, I miss the way she used to brush my hair'. But I still miss her. And I have no one to talk to about it: how could anyone understand it when I couldn't understand it myself.

Staring up at the wash of stars so very very far away, I suddenly felt totally and utterly alone.

My mish-mashed thoughts were interrupted by a familiar yip-yap.

'Libby!' I scooped up the brown fuzziness of whimpering tail-wag. On discovering it was me that his charge had escaped to, a breathless Emil looked as if he'd just downed a shot of lemon juice. His eyes travelled from me, to the club entrance, the story unfolding.

'Can I have my dog back?' He wouldn't look at me as I handed her over.

'She smells funny,' I said, in an attempt to fill the awkward silence.

'She had fleas. I gave her a bath.'

'Fleas only live on blood,' I offered. 'Like vampires.'

'Yeah,' he said, sighing. 'Like vampires.'

We looked at each other for a second before our eyes bounced off to catch details of the street: a loved-up couple dropping keys, laughing together in tipsy French, a stray bat sweeping low, and in the distance, a siren. Someone, somewhere, was in trouble.

'Hey,' I smiled hopefully. 'There's a retrospective of Stanley Kubrick films showing next weekend. Wanna come with? We could get spooked in *The Shining*, watch *Eyes Wide Shut* wide-eyed—'

'I'm busy.' He cut me off with the efficient detachment of someone unwilling to give spare change. 'Later, Mia.'

'Emil, wait,' I blurted, grabbing his arm as he turned to leave. 'Let's not do this.'

'Do what?'

'Pretend we're not friends!' I exclaimed. 'I'm totally sorry about Justin, but that doesn't mean I don't want to be your friend!'

He looked at me evenly, and I saw oceans behind those green eyes, eyes the same colour as mine. 'But I don't want to be yours.'

16

Have you ever noticed how sexual girl-tool ads are? 'Buy this scrub for a deep *penetrating* clean', or 'This conditioner *penetrates* the hair follicle'. Are we more likely to cough up for stuff if we're subconsciously thinking it'll get us laid? Making yourself look and smell good is so not the hard part. Finding someone to do it with who you *won't* regret every time the question of 'so who did you lose your V-plates to?' comes up at every sleepover from now till eternity, that's the doozie.

My mind was on important matters such as these when Rocho asked me to stay back after class. Irritation hung round my head like a cloud of buzzing bees. Fantastic, now on top of everything else, I'd be late for rehearsal.

'I have to be somewhere . . .' I began, as the other kids drained out the classroom door.

'Your essay on art practice in contemporary Australia,' Rocho gestured to the paper in front of him, 'I'm going to have to fail you on it.'

I stared at the assignment with little surprise. It had been due a few days before the Battle of the Bands heat and most of the time I'd allocated to studying had been spent trying to stop Lexie multi-slacking with her phone and junk food and start learning her parts.

'Oh,' I said. 'How unexpected.'

'Mia, I'm going to be blunt,' Rocho begun. 'It's clear you're not applying yourself in this class. However, you do show potential. You have your dad's eye when it comes to composition—'

'I'm not my dad.' I interrupted. 'Though it'd probably be easier for everyone if I were.'

Rocho regarded me as if I were a painting he didn't quite get — *what were the artist's intentions here?*

'The painter has only to create one masterpiece — himself, constantly. Your friend Yves Klein said that,' he commented. 'And his father was a painter too.'

'Wild,' I muttered, inspecting my cuticles.

'Mia, is there anything stopping you from applying yourself in this class?' he asked, giving me a 'meaningful' look. 'Anything you want to discuss with me?'

'No.' Yeah, I'm gonna spill my guts to a teacher. The delusion was almost sad. 'I really have to be somewhere . . .'

'I can't keep you in this class if you don't want to be here,' he said matter-of-factly. 'Your presentation at the end of term exhibition this Friday will be the deciding factor as to whether—'

'This Friday?' I interrupted, suddenly alert. 'As in, *this* Friday?'

'We've asked your father to be the guest speaker. The letter should arrive today.'

My mind reeled. 'But that's . . .'

'The same night as your band final,' he finished pointedly. 'You have a decision to make Mia. Your band, or your future here at Silver Street High.'

'What?' I exclaimed. 'That's crazy! I thought the point of this school was to encourage students to pursue creative stuff, not punish them for it!'

'Yes, Mia, it is . . .'

'What about the kids who keep missing classes for those artists' residencies overseas, you're not kicking them out!'

157

'Those students applied for leave through the proper channels,' Rocho stated firmly. 'Yes, we tailor your curriculum to allow for creative advancement but that does not mean you can come and go from class as you please. We will treat you like professionals on the provision you act like professionals. And not informing me about your band final being the same night as a class presentation is not professional behaviour at all.'

'But, that's not fair . . .' I whined.

Rocho looked at me with absolute finality. 'Welcome to the real world, Mia. I hope you make the right decision about your future.'

'Dad? You home?' I called through the house, hoping today was one of his dawn til dusk art-making marathons. Grabbing the mail, I cycled through it – something official-looking from the Guggenheim, my scarily thick mobile bill from Optus, nothing from school. Panicked, I began shuffling through the art magazines, glossy catalogues and unread cookbooks that lived on the kitchen bench. I *had* to find the letter inviting Dad to speak before he did.

'Hello, pet.'

I jumped. 'Hey! I, uh, I thought you'd be working.'

'Are you looking for something?' Paint smudges coloured one cheek a bright blue.

'No . . . I mean yeah,' I replied, flustered. 'I was looking . . . for this!'

He frowned at the book I brandished triumphantly.

'Surely *Home Cooked Roasts Made Easy* flies in the face of your years of vegetarianism, pet.'

I blinked, a stupid smile slapped to my face. 'I wanna

keep my options open. Okay, I better go . . . read this book then . . .'

'I thought you might be looking for this.' He held up the letter from school. My mouth went dry and my hands went clammy.

'Oh yeah.' I swallowed uneasily. 'I was totally meaning to tell you about that . . .'

'Mia, I know exactly what's going on.'

'You do?' Foiled . . . by Rocho! Curse him! 'I can explain . . .'

'Pet,' he started gently, 'I understand if you don't want me to speak at your school event. The idea makes you uncomfortable, doesn't it? I don't want to steal your lime-light—'

'No, no, it's not that,' I interrupted. 'It's just . . . I can't go to that.'

He stared at me uncertainly. 'You can't go to your first exhibition?'

'Yeah, the thing is . . .' I coughed, my mind racing. 'I promised Seb I'd babysit Theo that night, and he's really counting on me . . .'

'Oh, Mia, don't be ridiculous!' Dad chuckled. 'Seb can find someone else.'

I waved my hands about dismissively. 'Look, it's just gonna be a bunch of dumb kids from class talking about how abstract expressionism is dead and trying to suck up to you. It'll be upsetting for both of us.'

Dad frowned at the letter. 'It says here attendance is compulsory to pass the term.'

I nodded thoughtfully. 'Technically yes, but—'

'Then that settles it!' he interrupted incredulously. 'You're going and that's final.' He turned to retreat to the safety of his studio, where tubes of blue paint didn't offer any resistance to his will. Panic rose in me. The time had come. I had to truthenise.

'I can't go because I'm in a band and we're playing that night.'

Dad stopped in his tracks. 'What?'

'I'm in a band, with Lexie and Seb. And we won our school Battle of the Bands heat and we're playing the State Final this Friday.'

'You're in a band, and you never told me?' He looked totally baffled.

'Only because you'd never let me,' I replied indignantly. 'And . . . I'm kind of failing art.'

He blinked, mouth opening and shutting like a contestant on *Candid Camera*.

'Yeah, I know.' I sent my eyes skyward. 'You're not mad, you're just disappointed . . .'

'Wrong, Mia.' His voice was scarily low. 'I *am* mad. I'm hurt and disappointed, but I'm also mad. You keep secrets from me, you lie to me! What happened to my daughter?'

'I don't need this.' I grabbed my satchel.

'Don't you go anywhere!' Dad yelled, and I jumped.

'Don't yell at me!'

'I'll do whatever I damn well please,' he shouted. 'That seems to be how things are going around here!'

'You always said I could do whatever I put my mind to, and now I'm doing it and you're mad at me?' I snapped, blood racing. 'Nice double standard, Dad.'

'That doesn't mean failing school!' His fingers dug into his temples. 'Or lying to me!'

'That's because you don't think what I like is worthwhile! Do you know how humiliating that is?' My voice rose. 'Don't you get it?' I grabbed the letter and began ripping it up, my voice now a scream. 'I hate it! I hate all of this! I'm sick of being your daughter!'

He looked at me as though I'd just punched him in the stomach.

The tears that had threatened to spill now streamed down my cheeks in aching, heavy sobs. I turned and ran for the front door.

'Mia, wait!' he called, voice riddled with distress. 'Let's talk about this!'

I whipped round in the doorway, spitting words like bullets. 'You're fifteen years too late, *Sal*.'

17

'Okay. What do pecorino lovers consume?'

'Dude, you're making that up!'

'I am not, man. That's the question, "What do pecorino lovers consume?"'

'That's easy. Dudes with pecs.'

'Check-swish!'

A grotty lounge room piled with pale, pierced kids sporting shocks of black hair and legs skinnier than mine all laughed. Lexie jumped up to hug me tightly.

'Punks playing Trivial Pursuit?' I murmured as she let me go. 'Now I've seen everything.'

'Hey, Mia,' everyone chorused. 'Rad show last week.'

I managed a shaky smile. 'Thanks, guys.'

Lex sussed the red-eye factor instantly and grabbed my arm. 'Let's hang in Dice's room till he gets home.' She steered me down a darkened hallway, past ancient amps and skinny sleeping cats, and into a shoe-box bedroom dominated by a seen-better-days mattress propped up on milk crates.

She closed the door, eyes shooting questions. 'What's up?'

As we lay together on stinky sheets, I relayed my tale of woe: Nikki's cameo on my date with Justin, the fallout with Emil, the massive fight with Dad, the fact I was failing art . . .

'Oh man, I hear that,' Lex sighed. 'I'm failing everything except English. And I'm only reading *Hamlet* so I can pay Sissy out via Shakespeare.'

'For real? Even Dance?'

'You can't eat whatever you want and still fit into those leotards,' she replied bluntly. 'I'm not into it.'

'What are you gonna do?' I asked, suddenly worried. Life without Lex? 'They'll kick you out.'

She shrugged. 'I'll work something out. C'mon, back to you. After you went back inside the club, what happened?'

'He got drunk, and paid for me to catch a cab home.'

She narrowed her eyes. 'And Nikki? Did they hook up?'

'I don't know,' I admitted.

Lexie sat up straight, adopting her warrior woman tone. 'No way, dude. *No way*. He's your guy and you have to fight for him!' A familiar twinkle skipped into her sky-blue eyes. 'I have a plan!'

'And it involves a failed attempt at sneaking into a club, right?' I knew that twinkle well. 'I don't know . . . Maybe I should just wait for him to call.'

She shoved me playfully. 'C'mon Mia! You're in the final two! And true love is totally worth fighting for.'

'Well, you're the expert on true love,' I teased. 'You're here all the time! Bow chica bow bow . . .'

But Lex was shaking her head vehemently. 'Oh no — I learnt my lesson there. I don't believe in love, remember?'

I rolled my eyes. 'Whatever, Miss Martyr. Spill!'

Lowdown: Dice was the older brother of Matt, the bass player in The Boners. He was eighteen, had seven piercings, five tattoos and, naturally, worshipped the ground Lexie strutted on.

'It was lust at first sight,' she confirmed with a grin. 'But the trick is, don't get too close. As soon as you become a sure thing, that's when the magic goes.'

'Oh man, is she on that trip again?' A mohawked boy with spiked green hair stood in the doorway, giving her an amused smile. 'Change the record, Lex.'

She stuck her chin out petulantly. 'This is *girl talk*, Dice. We need privacy. Go buy me some chocolate.'

He laughed, tossing his jacket onto his floordrobe. 'Are you always this bossy or are you just trying to impress me?'

'Shut up! You need to be impressing me!' She leapt to her feet to stand at the end of his bed, arms folded.

'Oh, yeah?' He grabbed her round the waist, lifting her easily and nuzzling her neck. 'Admit it: you're desperate to be my girlfriend.'

'Stop it!' she shrieked, giggling and wriggling from his grasp, dashing off down the hall. 'You wish!'

As Dice followed the impish blonde brat, I realised it was time for me to also take a stand. Who cared if school sucked, my dad hated me and Emil didn't even want to be my friend? I didn't need them – I could score a rock god. If Justin wanted sex and sass, I'd give him sex and sass. Three words, Nikki Moretti: *Bring it on.*

'Are you sure about this outfit, Lex. It isn't . . . a bit much?' I stood nervously around the corner from Baby, barely able to balance in three-inch heels. My eyes were heavy with make-up, hair big, neckline plunging, handbag small.

'You're totally zeitgeist.' Lex clapped her hands in excitement. 'You look hot!'

'I feel very *Pretty Woman*, *before* he shells out for her feel-good transformation.' My stiletto heel caught in the concrete and I almost stumbled. 'And I've realised that me and high heels were never meant to be.'

She squirted me with perfume. 'Let's go before you chicken out, McFly.'

Heads high, we made a beeline for the bouncer.

'Yo, I'm Justin's girlfriend,' I stated, channelling street-smart 'tude. 'He's expecting us.'

'And I'm the Stay Puft Marshmallow Man,' he deadpanned. 'So nice to meet you.'

'I'm serious!' I exclaimed, faking outrage. 'My *boyfriend* isn't going to be happy when he hears . . .'

'Lady, if I had a dollar for every chick claiming to be Mr Jackson's significant other, I'd be home in my jim-jams watching *The West Wing* with my wife. Get in line,' he gestured to the queue, 'and I'll need to see IDs.'

Our hearts sank. Was this really the end of the line? We were all but ready to admit defeat when a voice as smooth as butterscotch sauce simpered behind us. 'It's cool, Lou. They're with us.'

As if my day couldn't get any weirder, now our sworn enemies, Sissy and Stacey, were busting us into Baby.

'Let bygone be bygones?' Lexie whispered furiously to me as the twins sashayed out of earshot. 'I don't buy it for a millisecond. Those girls hate us!'

'At least we're in,' I replied, scanning the room.

'There he is!' Lexie's voice bubbled over with excitement. 'Alone at the bar!'

The sight of him still made me queasy with nerves: all slouchy, smoky sexiness, the loner in need of love. *My* loner. He smiled briefly at the bartender who refilled his drink, and I wanted so badly to be the one making him smile, to feel his leather-clad arms around me, his lips pressing into mine. Why was I so nervous? We were practically an honest-to-God couple. *My first boyfriend.*

I smiled at Lex, suddenly at peace. 'How do I look?'

She foofed my hair with the eye of an expert. 'Perfect.'

'Thanks for making me come tonight, Lex.' I hugged her hard. 'You're the bravest person I know, and I totally love you for it.'

'Aw, shucks,' she grinned, embarrassed. "Nuff of that. Go get your guy.'

I spun around and took a step in his direction, but as I did everything seemed to drop to a seasick slow motion.

In slow motion he smiled at someone across the room.

In slow motion the someone flicked her hair as she sidled up to him.

In slow motion he cupped his hand around her head, pulling her close.

In slow motion Nikki and Justin kissed as passionately as long-lost lovers, right there at the bar.

I staggered back as if thrown by an explosion, slamming straight into a tall brunette balancing a tray of cocktails. The glasses crashed to the floor, and Justin and Nikki's heads whipped up, locking eyes with me in shock. Nearby, Stacey and Sissy watched the scene with obvious delight.

'Mia?' he stuttered, disengaging himself from Nikki.

'You're a joke!' Lexie snarled at Nikki.

'Better than being a tramp!' Nikki spat back.

'I wanna go,' I mumbled to Lexie, feeling light-headed, sick. 'Let's just go.'

'Mia, wait!' Justin's eyes were bouncing between all of us, but Lexie shoved him, back with a growl.

'You stay away from her, you jerk!'

'Hey!' A bouncer towered over us, snatching at Lexie's arm. 'What's going on?'

Nikki sneered at us in satisfaction. 'You really thought

you had a chance with him, didn't you?'

'Shut up, Nikki,' Justin snapped, but she ignored him and took a step towards us.

'That's as pathetic as your lame-ass band.'

Lexie snatched a nearby drink. 'I think the town bike needs a change of oil!' she hissed, splashing the drink in Nikki's face to a collective intake of breath from the fascinated patrons.

'That's enough!' interjected the bouncer, but Lexie ducked out from his reach with a dancer's grace as Nikki gasped, dripping wet and furious.

'You're DEAD!' she screamed, lunging forward and smacking Lexie hard across the face.

For a second everyone stood stock-still, stunned. Then Lexie's jaw dropped and she emitted a monstrous yell and threw herself at Nikki in a blonde fury of flying fists. They both smashed through a table full of drinks, screaming, slapping and out of control. Bouncers swarmed to pull the wildcats apart, and a security guard dropped a heavy hand on my shoulder. Oh man. This really wasn't how my night was supposed to end.

Soundtrack: 'Low Happening', Howling Bells
Mood: Low

Every now and then your daily routine splits at the seams to give you an unexpected glimpse of a life you've never known. Like the time Lexie nicked her mum's credit card and shouted us high tea at a fancy restaurant that looked like something out of a movie, where a glass of champagne was ten bucks and everyone called us 'Ma'am'. Or when Seb took me to an anti-racism rally in the city and I realised not everyone's biggest problems were wayward rock stars and an inability to apply liquid eyeliner.

As the clock struck twelve, I should have been tucked in bed with a dog-eared novel and a hot Milo. But tonight I was trying to convince a wasted guy *called* Milo that I definitely, *absolutely*, was not a pixie.

'Are you shure,' he slurred, bleary-eyed and bloated, waving a fat finger at me. 'Not a shweet pixie?'

'How much longer do we have to wait?' I hissed to a bruised and battered Lex, who was busy shooting daggers at an equally bruised and battered Nikki, sitting across from us in the cop shop foyer. Alongside the busted drunks, dealers and dope fiends, we'd suddenly become extras in a cliché-riddled police drama: teenage delinquents 1, 2 and 3.

'This isn't over, Moretti.'

'Are you threatening me?' Nikki's voice rose in pent-up fury. 'Officer, this girl is threatening me!'

'Hey!' bellowed the cop on duty. 'I'm not gonna tell you two again — any more trouble and you'll both be waiting in a cell.'

His threat was, thankfully, enough to shut them up. I could barely keep myself together, let alone control Loose Cannon Lex. A planet-sized headache drummed into my skull, growing by galaxies every time I cast my mind back to the club.

'Lexie!' A distraught-looking Dice raced towards us, mohawk still perfectly intact.

'You came!' Lexie threw her arms around his neck, clinging to him for dear life.

'Of course I came.' He inspected her injuries carefully. 'Oh baby, you're hurt. You need to clean these cuts up straight away.'

'I feel better now you're here.'

'But they could get infected.' He took her hand seriously, their entire attention focussed completely on each other. I didn't know if I wanted to roll my eyes or burst into jealous tears. 'Is it cool if I go home and get you some supplies?'

'Only if you want to. But don't be long!'

As they kissed tenderly, Nikki snorted. 'Word to the wise, pal: enjoy the devoted lover routine while it lasts.'

Dice looked taken aback. 'What?'

Nikki stared at Lexie hatefully. 'Lexie's relationship expiry dates give milk a run for its money.'

Lexie rolled her eyes. 'Ignore her baby, she's concussed and a cow. I'll see you soon.'

As a psyched-out Dice made for the door, Lexie whipped round to Nikki, whispering furiously, 'Are you trying to ruin everyone's life now, Moretti?'

Nikki stared back at her incredulously. 'You really have no idea why I have a problem with you, do you?'

Lexie threw her hands in the air. 'Finally, a revelation! I was under the impression we were BFFs, until OMFG . . .' She paused, suddenly stuck. 'Until . . .'

Nikki smiled grimly. 'Until you ditched me for Sissy and Stacey.'

Lexie frowned. 'No, I didn't.'

'Yeah, Lex, you totally did,' Nikki sighed. 'You stopped returning my calls and started partying with them every weekend.'

Lexie's mouth went slack. 'But . . . you were so busy being a sports queen . . .'

Nikki laughed sourly. 'Better than sitting alone at lunch, right?'

Lexie shook her head, confused. 'No, but . . . it wasn't on purpose . . . I mean, I didn't realise . . .'

'I know.' Nikki leaned forward intensely. 'That's what hurt the most. You were my best friend, you dumped me and you *didn't even realise*. That's what you do, Lexie. You ditch people and genuinely don't care.'

'But, I didn't mean to . . .'

Nikki simply shrugged. 'But you did.'

Lexie stared at the scratched lino at her feet, and I watched the memories of her past shatter, pieces of a puzzle she would have to rebuild. 'Nikki, I . . .'

'Alexandra Cannon, Mia Mannix, Nicole Moretti?' A police officer snapped our attention back to the problem at hand.

'Yeah, um, yes, sir?'

'The owner of the establishment has decided not to press charges.' As we breathed a sigh of relief, he held his hand up. 'However, given that you are underage, if we catch you on the club's premises again not only will you face serious consequences, but the club will lose it's license. Do I make myself clear?'

We mumbled our agreement.

In a tone bordering on disappointment, he concluded, 'You're all free to go.'

Outside we stood in an awkward trio, unsure of what the night's events and revelations meant.

Nikki broke the silence. 'Look, Lex, I feel better now I've had my say and stuff, but this isn't a Kodak moment. I don't wanna go back to being besties or anything.'

'Yeah, cool,' Lex said with obvious relief, as Dice pulled up in his beat-up old Ford. 'I think we're both, um, pretty different people now.'

'And I'm sorry you had to see me and Justin together,' Nikki said to me, guardedly. 'But I'm really into him, so I'm gonna keep hooking up with him. You can do what you want.'

I nodded. With a final goodbye glance at both of us, she turned and disappeared into the night.

Dice loped over to us, bearing medical supplies and a cheeky grin. 'The doctor is in. You want me to help with the bandages then drop you home?'

Lex drew in a deep breath, glancing at Dice somewhat sheepishly. 'Maybe I could stay at yours tonight. That's what girlfriends do with their boyfriends, right?'

There was only the slightest flicker of surprise before he drew the tired wild child into his arms. 'Yeah. That's what they do.'

As they gazed at each other in quiet adoration, I realised Lex was right. If a former goody-two-shoes pampered princess could find happiness in the arms of a walking safety-pin, true love was worth fighting for. And I sure had a fight on my hands . . .

Soundtrack: 'Work It Out', Dappled Cities
Mood: Finally working it out

His bedroom was as chaotic as his newspaper office. An intimidating number of books lined one wall, while a desk threatened to collapse under art supplies, familiar school texts and charcoal sketches. Weird black-and-white photos of industrial shapes were tacked above his bed, and everything from cereal box figurines to VHS copies of strange and lovely films littered the floor.

'Oh, *Eraserhead*,' I said nervously, picking it up. 'I love this film. Did you know it took David Lynch six years to make?'

'Can we cut to the chase?' Emil said simply. 'I know you're not here to discuss non-linear cult cinema. Plus I'm wearing Alf pyjamas.'

He was, but I couldn't. 'Yeah, six years. That's a long time, huh? You'd have to be really sure you wanted something pretty badly to spend that amount of time on it. What if you were wrong? I mean, it's six year—'

'Mia!' Emil interrupted, exasperated. 'It's the middle of the night! What's going on?'

'Okay. Okay.' I shook my head to clear my thoughts, realising I really should have prepared an inspirational speech before heading straight over here. 'Before I came here, I was at the police station . . .'

'You're on the run?' His mouth dropped open in amazement. 'Did you kill someone? Did *Lexie* kill someone?'

'No, no, Lexie and Nikki just got into a crazy catfight at a club,' I began. 'Wait, that's not the story. At the police station Lexie's new guy, Dice, came to pick her up and she had this "realisation" . . .'

'Wait, she's with a guy called Dice?' Emil laughed. 'What is he, like, a punk rocker with a mohawk and a gazillion piercings?'

'Yeah, you know him?'

'I was kidding. Are you kidding?'

'About what?'

'About Mice. I mean, Dice . . .'

'Emil, I screwed up!' I blurted out. 'I picked Justin and I should have picked you.'

Suddenly, two people never short of conversation had no words at their disposal. Emil stared at me in astonishment and I stared back, equally surprised at the confession that had unexpectedly raced out of my mouth. Confused, I sank down onto his floor, pushing my fingers through the thick, comforting carpet. After a second, he joined me.

'My life has been pretty crazy since I moved here,' I started cautiously. 'I've had to make a lot of choices. Sometimes — okay, often — I've made the wrong ones.'

He leant back against his bed, listening.

'Around Justin, I was always so nervous,' I thought aloud. 'I thought I wasn't cool enough or hot enough or rock enough. But around you, it's like I don't have to pretend. I can be myself — even if I don't know who that is at the moment.'

He stared at me thoughtfully, not saying a word. Did he think I was an idiot? Pathetic? A two-faced troublemaker who couldn't make her mind up?

'Emil, I can't take back what happened, but if I could do everything different I would, in a second,' I said honestly. 'Please. I really think I deserve another chance.'

He smiled at me self-consciously. 'So, you're up for some stargazing?'

'Yes!' I exclaimed eagerly. 'Yes, we can go tomorrow, or . . .'

My voice trailed off as he leaned over me to grab the cord of his lamp. He switched it off with a quick flick, and suddenly we were surrounded by stars: hundreds of tiny glow-in-the-dark stars, stuck high on his ceiling, transforming the darkness. It was magical. I let my head fall back against the edge of his mattress to take them all in. I wanted desperately to be a regular fixture of this comfortable, fascinating room – gazing at the stars, doodling on the floor, kissing in the doorway. I glanced over at the boy I wanted so badly, his calm, soft, mysterious energy now seeming closer than ever.

Slowly, almost without moving any other part of his body, he let his fingers inch towards mine. An electrifying shiver raced through me as he took my hand into his. The most intimate moments in the world don't happen in night-clubs or backstage or even on the movie screen. They were moments like these: sitting silently, comfortably, holding hands on a darkened bedroom floor.

'I still think about you,' he admitted.

I smiled with relief. 'Me too. When I saw Justin and Nikki together tonight, all I wanted was . . .'

'Wait – what?'

'Yeah.' The playback evoked bitterness. 'Leopards don't change their spots and apparently neither do lame, horny rock boys . . .'

His fingers dropped from mine. 'So, you're here because Justin dumped you?'

'No!' And suddenly the mood was broken. The soundtrack had changed from romance to danger, and we were no longer lazing in a river, we were fighting against a current. 'No, it's not like that.'

His face filled with an awful look, voice strangled. 'But if they weren't, would you still be here now?'

My mind raced, I didn't know. Would I?

'I can't believe you.' He ran his hands through his hair, flinching as I reached out to grab them.

'Emil, wait, I didn't mean that . . .'

'I'm not your back-up plan Mia!' he yelled, flicking on the light. 'I'm not some second-best boyfriend you can run to when . . .' He breathed out tensely.

The truth hit me hard: I had just made a huge mistake. Tears banged on the doors to my eyes. My throat constricted, my words choking, childlike. 'But, you're the one I want to be with, I swear. I promise!'

He moved swiftly to open his bedroom door, turning to look at me with dreadful conviction, eyes cold and hard like dirty ice. 'I think you better go.'

Choking with tears, I ran. Down the stairs, out of his room, out of his house, gulping for air, tears stinging my eyes and blurring my vision. I ran, I just ran.

19

Soundtrack: 'On Longing', Holly Throsby
Mood: Devo

My first memory of true, all-encompassing grief took place when I was seven, when my cheeky kelpie Elvis the Instigator had been found limp and lifeless by the side of the road. Now, almost nine years later, that feeling of sadness had once again taken my heart into bottomless darkness. But it wasn't Elvis the Instigator I had lost this time. It was love.

'Love? You were in love with Emil?' Lex stroked my hair suspiciously, curled up around me in my bed.

'I think so,' I sniffled, blowing my nose. 'If it hurts this much I must have been. I loved him and I blew it!'

'Maybe there's still a chance,' Seb hedged, staring at my ceiling. 'Maybe he was just angry . . .'

'You think so?' I sat up, staring at Seb with desperate eyes. 'Really?'

They exchanged doomed glances. 'Look, Mia, there's plenty of fish in the sea . . .'

I cut them off with a moan, and threw myself back onto a pillow already wet with tears. I felt worthless, stupid, ugly, cruel and any other negative adjective my bad brain cared to throw up. Everything – school, boys, the band, Dad – felt too hard. 'When did life get so complicated?'

Seb snorted. 'That's rhetorical, right? We're teenagers, baby. I read a study claiming adolescence was similar to a temporary insanity. Something to do with chemical imbalances.'

Lexie nodded. 'That'd explain emo.'

My voice quavered. 'Everything's falling apart.'

Lexie squeezed my hand. 'C'mon babe, you don't need a guy to be happy.'

'That's easy for you to say,' I whimpered crossly. 'You have one.'

'But before I didn't, not for ages,' she replied. 'And most of the guys I got with when I was a Star Sister . . .' She trailed off, shuddering briefly at a private memory. 'What a total waste of a perfectly good virginity.'

'Tell that to my raging hormones,' I sighed miserably. 'I can't stop thinking about him.'

'Maybe you're in love with the idea of love!' Seb snapped his fingers with panache. 'Maybe your brain is tricking you into thinking you like Emil, but really it's one of those want-what-you-can't have things.'

'Yeah,' exclaimed Lex. 'Like the time I bought all that stuff to make my hair curly, and then I realised I totally hate curly hair!'

'So, tell us what you actually like about Emil,' Seb instructed, sitting up. 'Honestly.'

I frowned. Maybe they were right. Maybe this was part of the trickery of girlhood. 'Well, he's definitely not as hot as Justin,' I began confidently. 'But he is cute, in that cool nerd-boy way. I like his glasses. And I like that he's tall. And funny. I like funny guys.' I paused, trying to let feelings about Emil slide naturally into my mind, like raindrops slithering down a wet window. 'I like that he sees the world as this fantastic place. Like all the stuff in his office, it's an alternate universe in there! He's kind and sweet without being drippy and pathetic – and it's totally cute how nervous he gets. I don't know, I just like that. He's fun to hang out with, and I can tell him anything.' I looked at my friends hopefully. 'So?'

'Right, that didn't go as planned,' Seb muttered.

'Fish. Sea. Heaps,' stuttered Lexie, glaring hard at Seb.

'She thinks it's cute he gets nervous!' He shot back at her. 'I had no idea she thought it was *cute* that he gets *nervous*!!'

'So, it's not a brain-trick?' I concluded weakly, bottom lip starting to tremble.

'Wow, is that the time?' Seb jumped off the bed hastily. 'I gotta jet. Lex? Ride?'

'That was supposed to make me feel *better*!?' My besties backed towards the door guiltily, as I tried to quell another rising flood of tears.

'We'll see you at the gig, babe,' Lexie tried to sound cheery as she grabbed her things. 'Nothing like a little rock'n'roll to lift your spirits.'

Flinging my door open, the two squeaked in fright as they bowled straight into Dad, who was about to knock. Mumbling confused hellos they tumbled off down the stairs together, the echo of the front door slam spilling through the house.

'Sweetie . . .'

'Go away.' I folded my arms, stony-faced.

'But, Mia, pet . . .'

'*Go away*!' I yelled.

'Mia, please tell me what's wrong. I can help . . .'

'You can help?' I laughed, once, hard, like I'd just been kicked in the stomach. 'You can't help me. No one can help me. No one even cares about me! You don't care about me, and Justin doesn't care about me, and Emil . . .' The tears started streaming down my cheeks. '. . . Emil doesn't care about me.'

I dropped my head into my hands.

'Oh, pet.' Instantly he was by my side, scooping me into a

big, soothing Dad-hug, and I started bawling in earnest. All the pain and humiliation and disappointment burst out of me in great heaving, gut-wrenching sobs and it felt like the end of everything.

Soundtrack: 'Happiness is a Chemical',
Darren Hanlon
Mood: Hung out to dry

Hot water hit tea-leaves and the kitchen filled with a strong, earthy smell, instantly grounding and comforting. Perched on a stool, wrapped like an invalid in a patchwork blanket, I watched Dad fuss around absent-mindedly — splashing soy milk into a glass jug, fishing out two pottery mugs from the dishwater, sniffing them sceptically before the artist's eye took over, and he held them up to admire their swirling blue-green colour.

I smiled wryly, flashing on a childhood punctuated by the scribbling of ideas in the supermarket, the admiration of sun on water triggering impromptu lectures on the art of the Impressionists, or the observation of amusing juxtapositions of people or street signs, usually to the annoyed yells from motorists backed up behind us, falling on deaf Dad-ears. He sees what he wants to.

'Tea strainer?'

'Second drawer.'

He smiled. 'I should spend more time in the kitchen.' Handing me a cup, he cleared his throat, trying to wrap his head around Girl World. 'So, there's no chance of a reconciliation with this Ian fellow?'

'Emil,' I corrected. 'Seb's 8-ball said it best: "Outlook not so good".'

He clucked at me sympathetically. 'You'll meet someone else, honey.'

'Let's eighty-six the clichés Dad. I'm not in the mood.'

He complied, as we sipped our tea quietly: warm, smoky Russian Caravan.

'This was your mother's favourite tea,' he said unexpectedly. 'She drank it all through her pregnancy with you.'

'Really?' Mum stories were few and far between, I gobbled them up like breadcrumbs in a strange forest.

'One time we even had it *in* a Russian caravan,' he recalled, smiling. 'We were in Tatarstan, I believe, travelling with some folk musicians. One of our travelling companions taught her to play the *balalaika* – a type of violin.'

'So she was musical too?'

'Oh, sure,' Dad replied. 'Picked it up instantly. Beautiful singing voice too.'

I sipped my tea, letting a look make the point. He got it, and sighed.

'Look, honey, I don't want to stop you from playing in your band,' he began carefully. 'I just want you to think about the consequences of doing it *right now*.'

'But it's happening right now, Dad,' I tried to explain. 'I had no idea we'd make it through to the final, but we have . . .'

'Is this something you're serious about? Something Lexie and Seb are serious about?'

'Yes,' I replied, relieved we were on the same page. 'Absolutely.'

'Well then, it sounds as though your band will still be there when you finish school, but if you choose to pursue it now, your place at Silver Street High might not be.'

I stared down at the curled brown tea-leaves floating

around the top of my cup. What fortune were they about to lay out for me?

'I just don't want you to make a choice you'll regret.' He kissed my forehead, before a sudden thought struck him. 'I have something for you – for your project.' He rummaged through his bottomless coat pocket to find a black-and-white photograph. In it, a man was flinging himself – arms outstretched, eyes squeezed shut – from the second storey of a house out onto an ordinary, empty street below. *Yves Klein, 1960, Leap Into The Void.*

'Isn't he great?' Dad smiled fondly, as if Yves was an old friend. 'That's how I feel before I start a new work: about to hurl myself into the void, with no idea of where I'll land or what will happen. Exhilarating.'

A prickly shudder ran through me, summoning goosebumps up my arms. It was the first time he'd ever explained how painting made him feel. It felt significant.

My tea was cold by the time I made my decision.

Me, in a white room, alone. A single open window with no curtains and no glass lets the sound of traffic far below me spill in softly. I close my eyes and feel centred, whole, surrounded by peace, and bouncing, weaving pinpricks of light. I open my eyes and begin running towards the window, my feet racing over floorboards, my arms slicing through the air, my heart thumping in my chest. The window gets bigger as I get closer and I'm pushing myself off the floor, flying towards this window, and my feet hit the sill and push me off! In the brilliant blue sky beyond, air rushes past my face and my skin. I'm surrounded by nothing yet the whole world is enveloping me as I sail out, and finally, finally start to fall. Arms outstretched, hair flying back, I fall towards the earth.

But as the street below gets closer and closer, a wave of panic cuts up through me so fast it hurts. I realise I'm gonna slam straight into the concrete, limbs crunching, face smashing, total annihilation, no turning back, no way to stop, I can't slow down and . . .

Smack! Rocho's outstretched hand slapped Dad's eagerly, pumping it in an enthusiastic handshake.

'Thanks for coming, Mr Mannix,' he said, tone bordering on religious reverence. 'I know how busy you must be . . .'

'Oh, please,' Dad's hands danced dismissively, his visage exuding daggy affection. 'Anything for my girl.'

Outside, lighting flickered in the distance and heavy grey clouds rolled in from the sea. It was going to storm . . .

'We're all looking forward to the show.' Rocho, nodding keenly.

And then Emil entered the room, cool as a cucumber sandwich. A sharp shock hit me and I instinctively straightened, body tense. Would my presence unlock a glimmer of remorse, regret, a change of heart? The chance was Nicole-Ritchie slim, but it hung in the air as his eyes slid toward me – then right through me, past me, away. I didn't even register. I slumped. Rocho's voice crept back onto my radar.

'Yes, Mia's take on Yves Klein's work should be very entertaining. Ah, here come your "paintbrushes" now, Mia.'

Half a dozen boys from class paraded over to us, a knot of nervous male energy.

'Alrighty then,' Michael grinned, all beer-breath and bravado. 'When do we get naked?'

I felt my phone vibrate. Seb's name flashed. I quickly switched it off. 'Wait over by the side,' I instructed, with faux-confidence. 'I'll just get the canvas.'

I slunk off, desperate to find a quiet corner to hide in, or even better, a piece of floor to sink into on a more permanent basis. As my dolled-up classmates and their proud 'rents milled round the small gallery scarfing gooey camembert and salty black olives, I tried hard to focus.

Look, we were never gonna win. We'd enter again next year. We'd be more prepared then, have more of a fighting chance. I'd say I still wasn't over the Emil sitch (true). I couldn't face Justin and Nikki (also true). Dad would ground me – no, threaten to disown me – if I failed art class (not really true).

I squeezed my eyes shut and groaned. I was a coward. A

pathetic, pathetic coward. Across the room, embarrassingly signing books for people, Dad caught my eye and waved. I faked a cheery smile — he seemed so damn happy we were there together. After being such a brat all semester, I owed it to him to put on a brave face. Pulling myself together fiercely, I grabbed the huge white canvas and strode purposefully in the direction of my six human paintbrushes.

The applause for Sarah's explanation of a woman's reproductive system constructed only from Kraft singles — 'The Right To Cheese' — was dying down as Rocho began introducing my presentation. I checked my watch, 7.30 p.m. The first band would be onstage. I flashed on the hot blinding stage lights, the swell of applause, the pre-show adrenaline rush . . .

'Mia?'

'Yeah!' I jumped up, flushing cotton-candy pink. 'Um, boys?'

To a volley of whistles, gasps and giggles, my six paint-brushes paraded out, all dressed only in their underwear, pale flesh dripping with blood-red paint.

'Yves Klein threw himself into the void to create his art — literally and metaphorically,' I began, glancing at Dad. He beamed back encouragingly. 'Another great artist — my dad — told me that's how he feels before he creates his work, so I know Yves wasn't just drunk on *vino rouge*.' The class tittered. 'Creating art should be exciting, risky — it should make you feel alive. It should make you feel like you're throwing yourself into space and it doesn't matter where you land, because the process itself is as important as the outcome. And that,' I gestured at the boys. 'And that . . .' Paint was dripping down their hairy legs in red rivulets as everything I had said repeated itself in my own head. The implication. The meaning. And finally, the undeniable truth. 'And that . . . and that is exactly how being in a band makes me feel.'

A ripple ran through the class as I stood frozen on the podium, my ears ringing. That was how Seb and Lexie and Fire Fire and making music made me feel. I couldn't deny it, any more than I could deny my own name. The human paintbrushes glanced over at me, unsure where this part of the presentation was going.

'I have to go.' My voice was barely a whisper, so I said it again, louder, as determination and something like destiny blossomed inside me. 'I have to go.' I backed away from the podium.

'Mia . . .' Rocho's tone was a warning, but I knew what I had to do.

'I'm sorry.' As the sea of faces began to blur, my eyes found Emil, sitting right up the back, his face unreadable. My heart hurt as I remembered the look in his eyes when I'd left his bedroom.

'I'm sorry!'

'What?' the boys exploded. 'Hey! We're covered in paint here!'

'Mia Mannix!' Rocho called as I ran for the exit and the noise level in the room started to grow.

'Mia,' Dad was saying. 'Mia, wait!'

A stack of chairs in my way split the room open with a violent crash, as I started to run.

Soundtrack: 'Crash Tragic', Operator Please
Mood: Frantic

Bolting through the front entrance I ran headlong into several latecomers. I spun round to get my bearings, and realised that the venue was at least twenty minutes across town in a car. *Damn!* As thunder rolled ominously in the distance, I started trying to flag down the cabs that whizzed past, but they were already full of Friday night revellers out to get liquored up and loose. *Dammit!*

'C'mon . . . c'mon!' I prayed aloud, as cab after cab flew straight past me. My feet pounded the concrete as I bolted, panic rising up in me – I'd never make it on foot!

Suddenly a car screeched up in front of me, passenger door flying open.

It was Emil.

We drove fast in silence, my nerves a wreck. I was sweating as Emil deftly overtook the cars in front. Inevitably pulled up by a red light, I swore furiously, and he shot me a sidelong glance.

'Calm down. We'll make it.' He checked the time. 'Probably.'

I stared straight ahead. 'No surprises if we don't. I've already screwed up everything else in my life.'

'Isn't that just part of your charm?'

The light turned green and I was jolted back as he floored it. Rock'n'roll.

'Hey, you can't park here!' the security guard yelled as we slammed up onto the kerb at the back entrance.

'I'm in a band,' I babbled, jumping out and pushing past him. He grabbed my spindly arm in a vice-like grip.

'Laminate?'

I struggled pathetically. 'No, no laminate . . .'

'*No* backstage entrance without a laminate. The bands are already inside, kid.'

'No they're not!' I yelled, panicked. 'Because I'm in one!'

'She's in Fire Fire,' added Emil urgently. 'They're on, like, now!'

'Nice try, but you'll have to pay for a ticket like everyone else. Now get that car out of here!'

Emil stared at me helplessly. I sighed. 'C'mon, let's do what he says . . .' Satisfied, the bouncer turned his back. I threw Emil a look and he nodded.

'Now!'

Ducking past him, we made a run for it.

'Hey!' the bouncer shouted. 'Stop! Someone grab those kids!'

'This way!' Adrenaline pumping, we raced up some stairs and into the labyrinth of the backstage area, past women with walkie-talkies and clipboards, roadies loading gear, randoms hanging out. Rounding a corner we ran headlong towards a couple of security guards, and skidded to a halt. They hadn't seen us yet.

Thinking fast, I threw my hands around Emil's neck, pulling him close in a faux-embrace. The two guards dashed straight past us. We disentangled. Was it somewhat reluctantly? No time to tell.

'C'mon!' We were definitely getting closer to the sound of girls' harmonies finishing sweetly followed by huge applause. The announcer's voice boomed out, 'Thank you Koori Magic. And our last act for this evening, Silver Street High's entry . . .'

'Through here!' Pushing open a heavy stage door, I ran in the direction of the voice.

'There she is!' I whipped my head round to see Seb pointing at me, and a group of people running towards me.

'I'm sorry,' I gasped, as someone threw a laminate around my neck while I shimmied out of my skirt and into the emerald-green dress Lex had made. 'I'm so sorry!'

'No time!' shouted Lex. 'We're nearly on! You got thirty seconds, Miz!'

Someone zipped me up and threw a guitar strap over my shoulder. As I turned towards the stage, I felt a hand on my shoulder, a quick kiss on my cheek.

'For luck,' Emil smiled sadly, turning to leave, but I couldn't let him. 'Wait.'

'What for?'

I shrugged helplessly, my heart racing. 'Me? Please?'

As roadies lumbered past us to set up our equipment, all the noise and the nerves fell away. Emil opened his mouth to speak. 'Mia, you know I like you. A lot. I just can't trust you any more.'

An arrow plunged into my belly.

Emil nodded at someone past my shoulder. Justin was leaning against the wall, wanker-king of all he surveyed. My stomach bubbled blue-black – the sight of him made me sick with regret.

'No, Emil, it's not like that. I swear!'

The announcer called our name and a sea of hands began propelling me towards the stage. The gap between us widened. I stared at him pleadingly, overwhelmed with the need for him to believe me. This wasn't right, this wasn't how it should all end. As shuffling footsteps took me away from the person I felt connected to, I felt conscious of my body: heavy, doomed, a bird with no wings trying to fly but failing, flopping, ruined.

He shook his head, and I could only see, not hear, him say: 'I'm sorry, Mia.'

And suddenly I was onstage.

Soundtrack: 'He's Gonna Change', Fire Fire
Mood: #$%^&*!!!

Lexie sashayed out like a superstar, grabbing the mic confidently.

'Yo, you ready for a real rock show?'

The crowd roared their approval.

Lexie cupped her hand behind her ear, in mock-bewilderment. 'Are we in a nursing home here? *I said . . .*'

As Lex began her 'rev-the-crowd-up-to-the-point-of-explosion' act, I glanced down to the faces in the front row, head still whirring, and was stunned to see: 'Dad?'

He couldn't hear me, but there he was, right up the front, gazing up at me, expression indefinable. I stared back in fear, frozen to the spot. Running out of my exhibition and probably getting kicked out of school, that's gotta take daughter-disappointment to a whole new level . . .

Then the blinding white stage lights lit up in full, blocking out any view of the crowd, and Dad disappeared into darkness.

I took a deep breath and focussed, feeling my feet on the floor, the guitar over my shoulder, the heat of the lights, the energy from the seething crowd surging up and possessing me. I couldn't think about Dad now. I couldn't think about Emil now. Pure pleasure raced up my spine. It was time to rock.

Seb was waiting, sticks high, ready to count us in. He grinned at me, wired, psyched. 'Let's do it!' he shouted, 'One, two! One, two, three . . .'

Everything except the band evaporated from my mind as I felt completely connected to Lexie, to Seb, and to the people in the room. Seb's yell rung in my ears. '. . . Four!'

We were off!

'So you just bailed?' Lexie was gasping, eyes dancing madly. 'Leaving all those naked guys there?'

'Uh-huh,' I nodded, similarly breathless, slugging water thirstily, fading applause ringing in my ears.

'You're crazy.' Seb grabbed the water from me. 'I'd have stayed.'

'Wild,' Lex laughed, high on performance and bouncing off the walls. 'WILD!'

My head spun as I came down to earth backstage. I could feel dozens of unfamiliar eyes gaze at our hot, sweaty trio with curiosity, awe, jealousy, pride, but I wasn't ready for any of it. I needed my crew close. After something so furiously magical, having to re-enter real life was confusing. Adrenaline was still pumping through our blood like racing wild horses, and I felt exhausted and alive, ready. But for *what*?

'Mia.'

'Dad!' The last time I'd seen him look so out of his element involved a MacBook and MSN. I exhaled slowly as Seb and Lex shot me doomed looks. I'd played the music – now I had to face it.

Steering him out of the thick of the backstage storm, we faced off against a brick wall covered in scratched graffiti. I felt trapped – the truth had just been paraded in front of everyone I knew. I had nowhere left to run.

'Dad, I'm sorry, it just happened. Ground me – six months, a year, I don't care. I'll start at another school, or drop out, get a job . . .'

'Mia, calm down.' He took a moment to take me in, to reassess who I was in this completely new context, a context that had absolutely nothing to do with him. His eyes glistened.

'You sounded amazing up there.'

'Really?'

'You can really play . . .' Jeez Louise, the man was tearing up. 'I've handled this all wrong, haven't I?'

'No, Dad, I'm the one who lied . . .'

'I should never have made you sell your guitar. I'm so sorry, pet,' Two pink spots coloured his cheeks. 'You looked so wonderful up there . . .'

'Thanks, Dad.' I wrapped my arms around his neck in a hug, giddy with relief.

'And don't worry about school – we'll deal with what happens there.' He squeezed my shoulder, looking me right in the eye. 'Don't think you're getting out of a grounding, but from now on, we're a team, okay?'

'Okay,' I whispered.

Cutting off what could have turned into a full-blown *Oprah* moment – I was at a gig after all – I pulled myself back into character. 'Now enough with the man-tears. So not a good a look backstage.'

He smiled, pulling out a handkerchief to blow his nose. 'I better let you get back to it. All the kids here look so groovy . . .'

I opened my mouth to cut off his dismal attempt at Teen Speak, and realised he was joking. 'Trendy, Dad. The word you're looking for is *trendy*.'

'Good luck, pet. You really do deserve to win.'

As he turned to leave I felt a little teary myself. He drives me crazy and he's total fruitloop, but man, I have to say it, I kind of love my dad.

'All band members should be side of stage!' an organiser on way too many Red Bulls was shouting. 'The winner will be announced in five minutes!'

Backstage was buzzing. Dozens of bustling band kids sporting experimental haircuts and ironic second-hand T-shirts chatted and checked each other out, playing it cool, enjoying the ride.

Scanning the crowd for any sign of a tall lanky boy with glasses, I waved hello to Trick and Kien, exchanged compliments with some cute, curly-haired indie boys wearing Cons and cardigans, and found myself feeling part of something, something bigger than just me, Lex and Seb. We had a scene, a community. And it felt pretty damn sweet.

'First of all we'd like to thank all the bands . . .'

As the organisers began their spiel, I squeezed in between Lexie and Seb near the front of the stage, clutching their hands in mine.

Seb adopted his 'responsible' tone. 'Look, guys, if we don't win . . .'

'Heads will roll,' Lexie growled. 'Heads will freakin' *roll*.'

'And now the moment we've all been waiting for.' A hush fell over the auditorium as a crisp cream envelope was passed to the front. 'The winner of the NSW Battle of the Bands State Final, who'll be going on to compete next week in the National Finals in Melbourne is . . .'

We held our breath. Dead silence filled the auditorium.

'Peggy's Temper from Gosford High School!'

What? The auditorium erupted as four girls on the other side of the stage whooped in excitement, throwing their arms around anyone in spitting distance.

'Recount!' yelled Lex. '*Recount!*'

We bundled her offstage to lick our wounds in private.

'Does this mean we suck?' Lex asked. 'I mean, that was an awesome performance and everyone hated it.'

'Hey, everyone didn't *hate* it,' I countered. 'Another band was just better than us.'

She gawked at me in total confusion. 'I just can't understand how that's possible.'

'Excuse me?' A cute floppy-fringed guy a bit older than us was hovering nearby, an overzealous smile lighting up his face.

'Yeah?'

'Hi. I'm from Modern Love Records. Loved the show. Loved it.' He shook each of our hands keenly. 'Lexie, right? Wow, what a performance. Mia? Great stage presence. Nice guitar accents. Really nice. Seb?' He took a little longer to let go of Seb's hand. 'Man, you're one of the tightest drummers I've seen in a long time, and you're all, what, in Year 11? Wow. *Wow*.' His enthusiasm was palpable, words stumbling out his mouth in excitement. 'I'm gonna cut to the chase. We'd be really interested in signing you guys for an EP. That is, unless you're already signed?'

'We're, uh, considering our options,' Seb piped up before Lexie could ask what an EP was.

'Here's my card.' The guy handed it to Seb, letting his fingers graze Seb's just so as he did.

'Jake?' Seb read from the card. 'Your name is Jake?'

'Jake Hall,' the guy confirmed, giving Seb one of *those* looks. 'Call me – about the band or, um, anything else.'

He turned and loped off, leaving us staring after him in amazement.

'Jake . . .' Seb repeated, meditating on the card, a weird little smile on his reddening face.

Lexie shoved Seb teasingly, giggling hysterically. 'You should see your face! Omigod! Boy love!'

Her words hit home and I suddenly remembered what I had to do.

21

Down two flights of stairs, through heavy doors, and out the back entrance. A roll of thunder threatened rain as I stared at the empty road. His car was gone. He was gone. I was too late, or perhaps I never had a chance in the first place. Why had I wasted so much time chasing after Justin?

'Baby.' And then, there behind me, the wanker king himself. 'Nice . . . ,' a none-too-subtle graze of my rack, '. . . show.'

'Justin?' I faked confusion. 'You totally shouldn't have followed me here.'

'Why not?'

'Didn't they tell you? It's a wanker-free zone. By the year 2020 we hope to totally eliminate wankers from public spaces.' I smiled tightly, brushing past him en route to anywhere-but-here.

'Hey,' he grabbed my arm. 'Let's talk.'

'What about?'

'Anything you like.'

'Sure, let's talk. 1. You're a loser. 2. I never want to see you again. 3. See points one and two.'

Unphased, he chuckled, lighting a cigarette. 'You're over-reacting.'

'Is that so?'

'Yeah.' He blew smoke up over my shoulder. 'You should do something to relax you.'

I snorted. 'Like what?'

'Like me.'

Stunned, it was my turn to laugh. 'You really are that arrogant, aren't you? As if I'd ever go out with you again.'

'I'm not talking about "going out". I'm talking about something a little more casual and a lot more fun.' He sucked the cigarette back, his inward breath causing the hot end to glow brilliantly, his dark gaze hypnotic and penetrating. I realised I was holding my breath, and let it out slowly.

'Oh Juzzy,' I murmured, seductively plucking the cigarette from his fingers. 'I've been waiting for this moment for so long.'

'Of course you have, baby,' he grinned. 'It's me.'

I held the fag up in front his smug, smarmy face and then let it fall to the ground between us, squashing it out with my foot. 'I'd rather be alone on a desert island living on poisonous berries than sleep with, date or even talk to a stuck-up jerk like you.'

I turned to strut past him, my head high. 'Oh, and Justin?'

He looked completely bewildered. 'What?'

'That you were punching above your weight. That's what people thought of us as a couple.'

A huge feeling of satisfaction washed over me like a waterfall, and it was all I could do to stop from skipping away from him.

Soundtrack: 'Recovery', New Buffalo
Mood: You'll see . . .

We'd played an awesome show, I'd made peace with Dad and annihilated Justin, but I still didn't feel like heading to the afterparty. I had to find a tall boy with glasses.

Spinning on my heel, I crashed straight into someone on the footpath behind me.

'Ow! Emil!?' He rubbed the jaw I'd just smashed into. My head whirled. 'I thought you'd left. Where's your car?'

'It's been impounded. Security and me are no longer BFFs.'

'I'm sorry, that's my fault.'

'It's cool . . .' He coughed, fidgety. 'So . . . I guess I kinda overheard your little tête-à-tête with Justin.'

'Oh.'

He regarded me carefully, low-key amusement creeping into his eyes. 'You're not really one of those "friends with the ex" kinda girls, are you?'

'Not when the ex makes Hannibal Lector look like Mr Nice Guy, no.'

'Good choice.' He grinned at me, and the air around us relaxed. 'So, how'd the gig go?'

'We didn't win.'

'But how did it *go*?'

I smiled. *This is why I like you.* 'It went great.'

Stray street lights splashed pools of yellow onto the empty road beside us, warm air heavy with the promise of rain . . . and more. The sound of distant chatter and cars textured the atmosphere, but it felt far away and out of reach. We were two people alone on a footpath, but we were enough to fill an entire galaxy.

'Nice dress . . .' He reached out to touch the emerald fabric.

I flushed. 'You like it?'

'Uh-huh.' He took a step closer, making me feel ragdoll-soft and warm throughout. 'Kinda appropriate too, because culturally, green is associated with regeneration . . . hope.'

His hand slid tentatively up to cup my shoulder. 'But in the case of traffic lights, and most relevant to current circumstance,' his other hand gently took mine, 'green has been known to indicate safe to proceed . . .'

We didn't even notice when the storm broke, rain drenching us both. Instead we pulled each other close as our lips met.

It was a kiss that said 'this is the start of something important'. In this kiss time was lost, readjusted and made new. It was the first kiss.

Warm rain dripped down my cheeks. I locked my hands behind his head, my voice shivery-low and full of truth in his ear: 'You're the only one I want.'

And when he smiled back at me, everything in the world made perfect sense.

Soundtrack: 'Wishbone', Architecture in Helsinki
Mood: The ending is just the start

'Sure Lex, *everyone's* been asking about you.' I rolled my eyes at Seb as he and I weaved our way to my locker, juggling a stack of new music textbooks, soy lattes and the phone.

'What did I tell them? Duh, the truth: that Dice knocked you up and you're hauling ass to a trailer park to raise mini Lexie–Dices.'

'Lice,' offered Seb drolly as I jerked the phone away from my ear to stop the high-pitched squeals piercing my eardrum. 'I'm kidding, McScreamy! How's life at fashion college?'

Day one of term two was brochure-sunny. Swarms of students spilled onto the green campus, creating a ruckus in the corridors that had been silent for the past two weeks. The nine o'clock bell rang as I fiddled with my locker combination.

'Nup, I have my first music class, well, right now,' I told her. 'Seb is mucho excited because he gets to see even *more* of me. Aren't you, Sebling?'

'I'm finding it difficult to contain myself,' he deadpanned, looking insufferably hip in a new suit and sunnies.

'Babe, I got another call coming through. Yeah, we miss you too. See you tonight – six p.m., Emil's giving us a lift so don't be . . .' But, of course, she'd already hung up.

'Hey, Jake.' I winked at Seb, who instantly blushed. 'Yeah,

Tuesday's fine. But can we approve these photos before they go out? The last ones made us look like homeless teenage vampires. And not in the good way.'

'Um, excuse me?' A shy-looking girl tapped me on the shoulder, her mousy brown fringe brushing big eyes, wide with confusion. Classic newbie.

'It's my manager,' I mouthed at her, as Seb popped a Chupa-Chup into his mouth and sucked.

'Sorry,' she muttered, turning to scurry off.

Woah. Hello. Déja vu much?

'Wait, hang on,' I called. 'I'll ring you back, Jake.'

I wove easily though boys on skateboards and girls trying to catch the eyes of boys on skateboards until I caught up with her. I stretched out my hand, and smiled.

'Hey, I'm Mia. Welcome to Silver Street High.'

Mia's Best Mix-tape Ever

The Grates: myspace.com/thegrates

You Am I: myspace.com/youamiofficial

Cut Copy: myspace.com/cutcopy

Red Riders: myspace.com/redridersmusic

teenagersintokyo: myspace.com/teenagersintokyo

The Emergency: myspace.com/theemergency

Young and Restless: myspace.com/youngandrestlessau

The Presets: myspace.com/thepresets

Soft Tigers: myspace.com/softtigers

Faker: myspace.com/fakertheband

Damn Arms: myspace.com/damnarms

Catcall: myspace.com/catcallmusic

Lost Valentinos: myspace.com/lostvalentinos

Youth Group: myspace.com/youthgroupmusic

The Red Sun Band: myspace.com/theredsunband

Expatriate: myspace.com/expatriateband

Midnight Juggernauts: myspace.com/midnightjuggernauts

Pomomofo: myspace.com/pomomofomusic

Howling Bells: myspace.com/howlingbells

Dappled Cities: myspace.com/dappledcitiesfly

Holly Throsby: myspace.com/hollythrosby

Darren Hanlon: myspace.com/darrenhanlon

Operator Please: myspace.com/operatorplease

New Buffalo: myspace.com/newbuffalomusic

Architecture in Helsinki: myspace.com/aihmusic

GEORGIA CLARK: 28, Pisces, easily amused.

Editor of Sydney street press music magazine *The Brag* for several years, Georgia now has the skills to make the best mix-tapes ever. That also lead to 'singing' in a 'band' called Dead Dead Girls, which proved that anyone with a funky haircut could be a 'musician'. After writing and directing a few successful short films and working as a producer in television, Georgia now has a couple of completely excellent TV shows in development. Her dream is to create the next *Buffy* or *Veronica Mars*. Watch this space.